Of Course He Pushed Him
& Other Sherlock Holmes Stories

Volume Two: Crossovers and Alternative Histories

By

Chris Chan

Edited by David Marcum, Derrick Belanger

and Ray Riethmeier

Paperback ISBN 978-1-80424-060-1
ePub ISBN 978-1-80424-061-8
PDF ISBN 978-1-80424-062-5

Published by MX Publishing
335 Princess Park Manor, Royal Drive,
London, N11 3GX
www.mxpublishing.co.uk

Cover design by Brian Belanger

List of Original Publication Dates and Venues

"The Adventure of the Specious Spouse," published in *Sherlock Holmes: Stranger Than Truth*, edited by Ray Riethmeier, Belanger Books (April 2021).

"The Adventure of the Villainous Victim," published in *Sherlock Holmes and Dr. Watson: The Early Adventures Volume I*, edited by David Marcum, Belanger Books (November 2019).

"The Chapel of the Holy Blood," published in *Sherlock Holmes and the Great Detectives*, edited by Derrick Belanger, Belanger Books (July 2020).

"Of Course He Pushed Him," published in *Mystery Weekly* (October 2019).

"The Outline of Mystery," published in *Sherlock Holmes: Further Adventures in the Realms of H.G. Wells, Volume One*, edited by Derrick Belanger and C. Edward Davis, Belanger Books (October 2021).

"The Search for Mycroft's Successor," published in *After the East Wind Blows: WWI and Roaring Twenties Adventures of Sherlock Holmes, Vol. II: Aftermath (1919-1920)*, edited by David Marcum, Belanger Books (September 2021).

Once more, to my parents, Drs. Carlyle and Patricia Chan

And to my USM escape room friends, who did so much to keep my spirits up during the pandemic:

Anjail Floyd-Pruitt

James Grossman

Bill Lent

Blake Wanger

Contents

Introduction

Volume Two: Crossovers and Alternative Histories

Introduction

Part Two: Crossovers and Alternative Histories

The Sherlock Holmes universe is iconic. There are few rooms in all of literature more well-known and detailed in the public imagination than 221B Baker Street. The major and minor characters in the world of Sherlock Holmes are so well-drawn that even characters that only appear in one story or have just a handful of lines of dialogue in the entire canon are now legendary. The Sherlock Holmes Universe is so memorable that thanks to fandom, it branches out into other universes. For years, writers have introduced Holmes to classic fictional characters and famous figures from history. Others have changed the Sherlock Holmes universe a bit. A few years ago, I decided to get in on the fun.

When I was a senior in college, working on writing a novel for my senior project, I reread the entire Sherlock Holmes Canon from start to finish. Along the way, a friend of mine was the victim of a very cruel and totally false rumor campaign that nearly crushed her, though thanks to the support of those close to her, she overcame the lies and graduated on time. As the situation passed, an idea suddenly popped into my head. Readers only had Watson's word for what happened at Reichenbach Falls in "The Final Problem." What if some villain, possibly one of Moriarty's henchmen, decided to spread a baseless rumor that Watson had actually pushed Holmes off the cliff? Nothing came of this idea for about a decade and a half, until I finally revisited the plot and turned it into a short story: "Of Course He Pushed Him." I submitted it to a few venues, all of which rejected it, until after several months, the periodical then known as *Mystery Weekly* (now *Mystery Magazine*) accepted the tale and published it in their annual Sherlock Holmes issue.

"The Adventure of the Villainous Victim" is from a Belanger Books anthology covering the earliest years of Holmes and Watson's partnership, which are largely ignored in the Canon. I did a little research, and discovered a fascinating real-life case from that era featuring a train, a brutal murder, and an investigator named George Holmes. Could the newspapers have gotten Sherlock's name wrong? I decided to insert Holmes and Watson into this actual case.

"The Chapel of the Holy Blood" was written for a Belanger Books collection where Holmes solved cases alongside famous fictional detectives in the public domain. In my story, Holmes pairs up with one of my favorite sleuths, G.K. Chesterton's Father Brown, to solve a particularly sanguinary crime that may or may not have a link to the supernatural.

The real-life crusading lawyer Mary Grace Quackenbos Humiston (1869-1948) was a remarkable figure. At a time when few women received law degrees, she defended many poor and downtrodden people, getting a woman who had killed in self-defense off of death row, solving a missing persons case that turned out to be a murder, and exposing a human trafficking and exploitation ring in the American South, among many other adventures. For her successes, she was nicknamed "Mrs. Sherlock Holmes." What, I wondered, would happen if her path crossed with the real Sherlock Holmes, and people thought they were really married? And so, for a Belanger Books anthology where Holmes worked with actual figures from history, I wrote "She Is NOT My Wife!" which was retitled "The Adventure of the Specious Spouse."

Sherlock Holmes' brother Mycroft is said to be so influential, that at times, "he IS the British government." In a Belanger Books collection set after the Great War, I wondered, what would happen to the government if Mycroft was no longer around? Could anybody replace him? And so, Holmes and Watson began "The Search for Mycroft's Successor."

Finally, for a Belanger Books collection featuring crossovers between Holmes and the world of H.G. Wells, I wrote "The Outline of Mystery." Wells gained much wealth and fame for writing "The Outline of History," a massive tome that claimed to cover the entire history of humanity. It was a controversial book, especially when a Canadian woman named Florence Deeks sued Wells, claiming he'd plagiarized her unpublished manuscript. This led to a lengthy legal battle that Deeks lost, though the allegations are still debated today.

What if Deeks came to Holmes for help, and his investigation led to interactions with other famous figures connected to the controversy?

These are the first six stories that I wrote featuring Holmes in alternative universes and meeting classic fictional characters and figures from history. They won't be the last.

–Chris Chan

Part Two: Crossovers and Alternative Histories

Of Course He Pushed Him

"See him?" Battlecruiser Barry jabbed a finger with a cracked, filthy nail at the pub window, pointing at the dignified-looking doctor hurrying down the street.

Florrie leaned forward, causing Battlecruiser to involuntarily recoil backwards. Six years earlier, when women of Florrie's profession were being slaughtered on the streets of Whitechapel, a rumor circulated that Jack the Ripper had come up to her, taken one whiff of Florrie's breath, and then run away screaming. A slightly nastier version of the rumor suggested that Florrie's halitosis had proved lethal, which is why the Ripper's reign of terror finally ended.

"Oh, I know him-- his picture used to be in the papers all the time. Not so much now that his friend's dead and he's spending all his time seeing patients instead of solving crimes." Florrie shuddered. "So sad about his friend. Such a brilliant man. Terrible that he fell off that cliff in Switzerland three years ago."

"Yes... fell..." Battlecruiser put special stress on the second word.

"What do you mean by that?"

"Mean by what?" Battlecruiser tried to look innocent. It didn't suit him.

"You were being very coy when you say "fell." Of course, it wasn't an accident. He went off the cliff because of his fight with that professor, didn't he?"

Battlecruiser shrugged. "Well, that's the official line."

Florrie scraped her chair forward, causing Battlecruiser to scoot further back. "That's what the doctor said in his account, didn't he? Don't you believe his story?"

A contemptuous sneer spread across Battlecruiser's face. "The doctor would want everybody to believe that his pal was killed by a master criminal who's conveniently also dead and can't defend himself."

"Are you saying that's not what happened?" Florrie looked incredulous.

"I've got a distant cousin who works at that Swiss hotel where the doctor and his friend stayed, and my cousin told me that the so-called good doctor was acting very shifty the day his friend and the professor died."

"No! I can't believe it!" Florrie made an effort to sound indignant, but it was obvious that juicy, scandalous gossip delighted her. "You think-- you're saying that the doctor pushed his friend over the cliff and into the waterfall?"

"Of course he pushed him. It's obvious, really. There's something not quite right with the doctor. You can see it in his eyes, he's a wrong'un, he is."

"What about the professor? Are you saying the doctor killed him, too?"

Battlecruiser shrugged. "Who knows? You know that the doctor was in the army in Afghanistan. Some men go a bit wrong after a war. And not to be too crude to a lady, but there was always something a bit amiss with his relationship with his... "friend." Not surprising it turned violent. I suppose they quarreled, the doctor shoved his pal, and perhaps he took care of the professor as well because that distinguished old mathematician witnessed the crime. Then the doctor came home and wrote that ridiculous story to explain away the deaths."

Florrie continued to express skepticism about the doctor's guilt, but still paid close attention to Battlecruiser's theories. It was obvious that the possibility that the doctor was a killer, possibly a double murderer, had latched into her imagination. By the time she finally left to go in search of paying clients, she was not only convinced of the doctor's guilt, but she was itching to spread her suspicions to everybody she met.

Battlecruiser smiled when he saw Florrie whispering to one of her colleagues. Truth is sluggish, but malicious gossip is quick as lightning. He knew that if he spread the rumor to all of the names on the list, in a matter of weeks all of London would be convinced that the doctor had shoved his best friend off a cliff and into a central European waterfall.

Battlecruiser checked his watch. He had just enough time to make his date with the scullery maid, Polly.

•••

"I never liked him. There was always something uncouth about that doctor. I never trust a man who writes about himself. There's something vulgar about that sort of self-aggrandizement." Mrs. Talmidge sniffed disapprovingly, and adjusted her cards in her hand.

Mrs. Dinell tittered softly behind her cards. "I always liked the doctor's stories."

"Pure sensationalism! That's what they are!" Mrs. Talmidge had read plenty of the doctor's stories herself, but she was not about to admit that to the members of her bridge group, especially now that she had publicly implied that the doctor was a cold-blooded murderer.

"Wherever did you get the idea that he killed his best friend?" Mrs. Opaline inquired.

"Oh... a <u>very</u> reliable source. Someone who knows a lot of secrets, someone who I trust <u>completely</u>." Mrs. Talmidge had heard it from her lady's maid, though she wasn't about to reveal that fact to her friends. Her lady's maid, incidentally, had picked up the story from Mr. Talmidge's valet, who'd heard it from the parlormaid, who'd been told the rumor by the scullery maid, Polly, though the parlormaid had been sworn to secrecy.

"You mark my words," Mrs. Talmidge declared, laying down another card. "The police will arrest the doctor any day now. I'd bet my grandmother's pearls on it!"

•••

"Oh, you <u>mustn't</u> go to that horrible man!" Mrs. Opaline pleaded to her cousin, Mrs. Wellner. "It's simply too dreadful to think about! I hear that there is a witness who actually <u>saw</u> him push that marvelous detective over the cliff, and that professor as well-- they say that he was jealous of his friend's success, I think. I couldn't bear to have that man touch me for a second! No, dear, you really ought to go this other gentleman in Harley Street to look at your throat. He's very talented, very respectable. I have his address in my handbag here..."

The doctor's wife was an affable woman, and she was rather surprised when her so-called friend Mrs. Wellner cut her dead in the street.

Running up to Mrs. Wellner, the doctor's wife tugged at her sleeve and cheerfully said, "Juliet? Didn't you see me?"

Juliet Wellner drew herself up to her full height (which was not very imposing, as she was a tiny woman), and with glacial hauteur replied, "I should consider it a favor if you would not approach me with such unwelcome familiarity, madam."

The doctor's wife was stunned by this frigid reception. "Juliet, what on earth has gotten into you?"

"I have no desire to continue any acquaintance with a woman who has chosen such a disreputable husband. Good day and goodbye." Mrs. Wellner flounced down the street, and the doctor's wife stared at her open-mouthed.

•••

"You can come in now, Inspector."

The Inspector cautiously crept into Superintendent Dilys' office. It was obvious that there was tension in the air, but the

Inspector wasn't aware of having done anything wrong. The Inspector was about to lower himself into the chair in front of his superior officer's desk, but Superintendent Dilys snapped at him.

"Don't sit down."

The Inspector remained standing.

"You know why you're here, of course."

"No, I certainly don't."

"Don't be a fool. I know you do."

"I assure you, sir, I haven't the faintest idea."

Dilys snorted and leaned back in his chair. "Then you're an even bigger fool that I suspected. It's about that shady pal of yours."

"You'll have to be more specific, sir."

"That bleeding writing doctor! The one with that meddling dead detective friend!"

"Oh, him. What about him?"

"Just so you know, we're starting an investigation into him, and if you try to warn him off, I'll see you stripped of your rank. You understand me?"

"An investigation? For what?"

"Murder, of course. The London underworld is buzzing. Apparently every pickpocket and prostitute knows for a fact that he pushed his... roommate off that cliff a few years ago."

The Inspector nearly choked. "That's utter bosh, sir!"

"Is it? Well, whether it's true or not, we have to look into it. It's dashed inconvenient for us. Especially since the murder didn't happen on British soil. If it turns out a murderer has been involved in investigations for over a decade, that could lead to some pretty awkward situations. The Home Office is already asking some sharp questions about that bludgeoning in Herefordshire five years ago. We had the victim's son dead to rights, and that bleeding know-it-all detective and his shifty doctor friend got the boy acquitted, didn't they? And that other medical man who died. Who the bloody hell dies of a snakebite in Surrey? That stinks of rotten fish to me. Well, I knew that pair was up to no good from the beginning, sticking their noses where they didn't belong. And you're hand in glove with them, aren't you? Are you a dirty copper, Inspector?"

"What? No! I'm not!" The Inspector felt his face turning crimson, as the volatility of the situation suddenly became fully apparent to him.

"Well, I don't trust you half an inch, you little rodent-faced plodder. You can consider yourself on desk duty until further notice, do you hear me? Now get out of my office!"

The Inspector stormed out of Dilys' office, trying to control his rage. The situation was blatantly unfair, and he was helpless to clear either his own name or his friend's.

●●●

"I'd like to try on that hat, please," the doctor's wife asked the milliner.

The milliner glared at her. "No."

"Why not?"

"We don't want your type in this establishment. This is a respectable shop."

The doctor's wife turned chalk white. "I assure you, I am a respectable woman. My husband is a doctor--"

"Oh, I know all about your murdering husband," the milliner sneered. "I'm sure he'll be on the gallows before the month is out. Now get out of here before I call a copper and have you thrown out!"

The doctor's wife hurried out, trying to keep her dignity. This was the fourth time in three days that she'd had a confrontation like that. But she hadn't told her husband. It would only upset him, she reasoned…

As she shuffled down the street, she felt the stinging sensation of a steadily worsening pain in her head. She had been getting so many headaches lately, she was starting to worry…

•••

By the end of the following week, the doctor was quite possibly the only man in London who hadn't heard the rumor that he'd pushed his best friend to his death.

It was therefore with great bewilderment that he noticed that he was being snubbed.

On Monday, he received a letter informing him that his invitation to speak at a medical conference had been rescinded. No explanation was given.

On Tuesday, an old friend of his from the army had politely but firmly refused to have a drink with him.

On Wednesday, three of his patients cancelled their appointments with him, and informed him that they were changing doctors.

On Thursday, the doctor lost four more patients, and he noticed that a friend of his wife and her husband hurriedly crossed the street when they saw him walking towards them.

Normally, the doctor would have wondered about the cause of this sudden coldness, but his mind was preoccupied with other matters. He was worried about his wife. She had been looking very pale and fragile lately. Her health had never been robust, but lately… there were signs detectable to an experienced medical man that she was under severe strain. He had tried to talk to her in the hopes that she would unburden herself to him, but she had airily refused to admit that anything was wrong.

And so, instead of wondering why he was rapidly becoming a social pariah, the doctor focused his attention to his wife exclusively on Friday, when she suddenly collapsed with a burning fever and a devastating migraine.

•••

Battlecruiser chuckled. "Thanks for the money, Colonel. I must say, this is one of the easiest jobs you've ever offered me. No safecracking, no rough stuff, just a little bit of rumour-mongering. Will this be a regular thing?"

The Colonel did not look up from polishing his gun. "I'm afraid, Battlecruiser, that this will be a one-of-a-kind project. Step one of my plan for total revenge."

"Are you trying to get the doctor hanged?"

"Certainly not. That would be too merciful for him. I've lost a bloody fortune due to him and his friend meddling in the Professor's affairs. I'd be a millionaire now, vacationing in my private chateau on the French Riviera if that precious pair hadn't interfered. So, I want him to suffer. But if you really want to hurt an Englishman, you don't kill him. You humiliate him, and the best way to crush a really respectable Englishman's spirit is to shatter his reputation. Men can hold their heads up high when they can excuse away their personal sins, but they crumble when people believe they did something they didn't do. By the time I'm through with him, his practice will be in tatters and he'll wish he had a noose around his neck."

"I wonder if his wife will leave him."

"I dare say you're right, Battlecruiser, but not in the way you mean. My spies say that the doctor's missus has taken ill, and I suspect that the rumour-mongering has played a part in her sad decline. They tell me she's had some sort of seizure, and may not survive the week."

Battlecruiser chuckled. "Dear me, how sad."

"Yes, isn't it a tragedy? The moment her coffin is lowered into the ground, you can start a new fleet of rumours, suggesting that the good doctor may have contributed to his wife's demise. Perhaps some rare, untraceable poison he discovered while serving in Afghanistan. Won't that be delightful?"

•••

Superintendent Dilys strolled into the Assistant Commissioner's office. He wasn't sure why he was being summoned, but he hoped it something to do with the promotion he'd been angling for over the last six months.

It took one glance at the Assistant Commissioner to inform him that he wouldn't be getting promoted anytime soon.

"Dilys! I understand that you've launched an investigation into that doctor."

"Yes, Assistant Commissioner, that's right."

"Well you're going to cancel it right away, you hear me? Call it off, and bring all your notes on the case to me so I can burn them. Understood?"

Dilys turned purple. "But... But... Why? Doctor--"

"That doctor has a very powerful friend, and if you don't back off him immediately, it's the chop for both of us. So leave him be. That's an order."

"But--"

"I don't have to tell you why or who, Dilys, that's none of your concern. Just call off your dogs, and leave the man be. Oh, and that sly little fellow, the inspector who looks like a drowned rat. You put him on desk duty, didn't you?"

"Yes, I--"

"Well, take him the hell off desk duty. Apologize and tell him he'll be getting an extra fiver in his next pay envelope as an apology. And don't ask me to explain myself, you're not going to get any answers. Now get the hell out of my office before I break you down to a constable!"

Superintendent Dilys limped out of the Assistant Commissioner's office, wondering what had just happened and why.

•••

The fat man folded his hands across his ample stomach and leaned back in his chair. He did not like to show emotion, but he permitted himself a very faint smile as he observed the extreme agitation on Battlecruiser's face. The fat man's associates, Geoffrey and Bertram, both enormous men (though unlike their boss, their bulk was entirely muscle), stood behind Battlecruiser, oozing intimidation from every pore.

"You let me go now!" Battlecruiser tried to sound tough, but succeeded only in managing a plaintive whisper. "You can't keep me here!"

"I can and will," the fat man replied. "I am not pleased with you, Mr. Battlecruiser. You have caused a great deal of distress for my late brother's best friend and his wife. By slandering a good man and destroying his practice, you have caused irreparable harm to a heretofore sterling reputation. Now, why would a low-level criminal like yourself do such a thing? You never crossed paths with my brother and the doctor. You have no reason to spread slander. Unless... someone put you up to it. I believe that it was either the Colonel or the dentist. Which was it?"

Battlecruiser writhed anxiously. "I'll never tell! He'll put a bullet right between my eyes, he will!"

The fat man sniffed. "No need to tell me. I observed your facial expressions as I named my suspects. It was the Colonel who organized this little plot. Thank you for confirming my suspicions, inadvertent as your help may have been. Now, explain to me why the Colonel has initiated this smear campaign against the doctor."

"I won't say!" Battlecruiser moaned.

"As you wish," the fat man sighed. "Geoffrey? Please demonstrate the Baadsgaard method on Mr. Battlecruiser here. Perhaps that will induce him to talk."

"Yes, sir," replied Geoffrey, who knew full well that there was no such thing as the Baadsgaard method. "Do you want me to use the water version or the fire version?"

Waving a pudgy hand, the fat man carelessly replied, "Surprise me."

"You can't hurt me!" Battlecruiser shrieked. "I'm a British citizen! I've got rights!"

The fat man drew a small box of chocolates from his waistcoat pocket, popped one in his mouth, and sucked on it for a few seconds before swallowing it. "For the purposes of this investigations, I _am_ the British government. I can order Scotland Yard to drop any investigation I desire, and I have the right to revoke the citizenship of anybody I wish for whatever reason I see fit, and I do so to you now. So now, dear fellow, you may officially consider yourself a man without a country. And therefore, you have none of the protections that the British citizenry enjoy. Geoffrey, I believe that this case justifies the combined fire _and_ water method, if you would, please--"

"Wait!" Battlecruiser shrieked and started blubbering. His next several sentences rolled out of his mouth rapidly. "The Colonel wants vengeance against your brother. He knows he's still alive. The Colonel's never forgiven your brother and the doctor for breaking up the professor's organization. It cost the Colonel a fortune, and he's out for revenge. He told me to start spreading the rumor that the doctor killed your brother, because that was the best way to bring your brother out of hiding. This was all a ruse to get your brother to re-emerge so the Colonel could kill him for real. When he ordered me to start spreading the rumor, I couldn't say no, could I? Could I? He'd shoot me dead in the street if I didn't follow orders. It's not my fault, sir, don't you see? I had to do what I did. Please don't hurt me, gov, please!"

Battlecruiser started sobbing uncontrollably. The fat man, who had no patience for tears, snapped after two seconds. "Stop your blubbering immediately!"

"Yes, gov. Sorry, gov." Wiping his eyes, Battlecruiser forced himself to stop crying, and lacking a handkerchief, blew his nose directly on the floor, to the horror of the other three men. "So, can I go now?" Battlecruiser asked hopefully as he got up from his chair.

"Go? Certainly not." As the fat man spoke, Geoffrey and Bertram took hold of Battlecruiser's shoulders and lowered him back into his chair. "You will remain here for another two hours, at which point my associates here will escort you onto the *Rialto*, which sets sail for New South Wales at dawn. I have no idea how you'll make your living in Australia, but that is really no concern of mine."

•••

The fat man and his younger brother, the detective, were sitting in the elder brother's room at his club. The detective puffed on a pipe, and the fat man wrinkled his nose and tried not to make his displeasure too evident. From the amused glint in the detective's eyes, his brother was not succeeding.

"Must you smoke that wretched thing?"

"My dear brother, you know that it helps me concentrate my decision-making processes."

"Humph. What's to decide? Just come back to life already and be done with it."

"It's not that simple, as you are no doubt aware."

"Nonsense. You can walk back into your lodgings at any time. You just don't <u>want</u> to return."

"Whatever makes you think that?"

"I believe that you've come to prefer life in the shadows."

"I find that it is infinitely more efficient to destroy a crime syndicate as an essentially anonymous figure."

The fat man ground his fist into the arm of his chair. "Need I remind you, that not only does the Colonel know that you still draw breath, but that your supposed death has been weaponized by your enemies to cause the very genuine demise of the wife of your best friend?"

The detective became very still and quietly put down his pipe. "There was no need to mention that."

"Because you'd rather ignore that discomforting fact?"

"No, dear brother, because I never stop thinking about it." The detective leaned back in his chair and placed the tips of his fingers together. "We've had bodyguards on them around the clock for the last few years. I thought that if the remains of the Professor's gang did decide to go after them, they'd go for a physical attack. I can assure you, it was a humbling and salutary lesson when I discovered that the Colonel had chosen to launch an assault against which we were completely defenseless- rumor and innuendo. A pair of weapons far deadlier than even the most high-powered rifle, especially in the wrong hands."

Grunting in agreement, the fat man added, "But there is a quick and effective way to disarm this weaponized rumor."

"Reveal that I'm alive," the detective replied. "Yes, at this point, it's the only way to completely and thoroughly lay waste to the ridiculous idea that my poor friend killed me! How absolutely disheartening it is to realize that London society, particularly its medical establishment and its so-called "respectable" classes, could be so credulous, so willing to believe the most respectable and reliable man in the world was a cold-blooded killer! Be thou as chaste as ice, as pure as snow, thou shalt not escape calumny, eh?"

"It's a miracle that the doctor hasn't had an inkling of the whisper campaign against him yet."

"No. And he mustn't. Taken on top of the sudden loss of his beloved wife, hearing that all of his medical colleagues and fair-weather friends are looking at him with suspicion might very well kill him. And I can't have that. No, to save a good man's reputation and his life, and to avenge the death of a golden-hearted woman, I must return to a notoriety I have never sought and do not enjoy."

"Excellent. When do you plan to return to the land of the living?"

"No time like the present, I suppose. The longer I put this task off, the harder it will be to resume my old life. Tonight, I rise from a watery grave and simultaneously smash the Colonel's remaining portion of the Professor's gang, and obliterate his vile web of slander as well."

"How will you make your reappearance? An interview in the papers? A speech to Parliament?"

"No, London's reporters will break the story. I shall let my friend tell more in one of his well-intentioned but ultimately overdramatic stories. I think he deserves the opportunity to reveal his own innocence to the world without realizing it. Of course, he'll need a bit of crime to make it a proper story for that very lurid magazine. He might as well focus the story on the Colonel's capture and arrest for that recent fatal shooting. I shall set a trap for him within the hour, and then allow my friend to know that I am still alive."

"Fair enough. What will you do? Knock on his door and reveal yourself?"

"A bit too simplistic for my tastes, dear brother. I think that I must make myself known a touch more quietly, but memorably. You know that I cannot resist a touch of the dramatic. I cannot just show up at the good doctor's doorstep, at least not as myself. I think that I shall introduce myself to my friend in a way that he will not recognize me at first. I have been working on a particularly convincing elderly bookseller disguise…"

The Adventure of the Villainous Victim

I have lost count of all of the occasions where my friend solved a baffling mystery where the official police failed, only to allow the legal authorities to accept all of the credit for the resolution of the case. In contrast, I believe that there is only one instance of a case where my friend desired public recognition for catching a killer, but he was denied it due to a fluke of chance.

In June of 1881, shortly after our initial meeting, Holmes and I took a day trip to Brighton to make some purchases at a new tobacconist's shop that had rapidly gained a reputation for having a special house blend of fire-cured pipe tobacco that had smokers all over London raving about its quality. After making some purchases that severely strained both of our monthly budgets, we walked back towards the Preston Park Station to take a late lunch at a nearby café before catching the three o'clock train back to London.

Our plans for lunch were interrupted when we heard a man's screams coming from the station. We sprinted in the direction of the shrieks, and soon discovered that they were coming from a ticket collector. I am the first to admit that I lack my friend's observational skills, but it did not take a pair of eagle eyes to determine what was causing the poor man's distress. Sitting on the ground five feet away from the ticket collector was another man, whose entire body was covered in blood.

23

While Holmes delivered a firm yet gentle slap across the hysterical ticket collector's face in order to silence his ear-piercing cries, I examined the blood-covered man. After a minute's study, it became apparent that the blood was not his own. It was a disturbing realization. I shook his shoulder until he finally turned his head and met my eyes. "Look here, my good fellow, do you know what's happened to you?"

He stared at me with glassy eyes until finally he responded to my question. "I... don't remember. Not everything, anyway. After they attacked me..."

His voice trailed off and I snapped my fingers in front of his face to keep his attention. "Listen, sir, please try to stay with me. I'm a medical doctor and I need to find out what's happened to you. You say you were attacked. Who did this to you? What did they do?"

"I don't know. After they struck me, everything's a blank."

My friend's voice made me jump. I hadn't expected him to join in on the questioning. "Perhaps you can start by telling us your name. If, of course, you can recall it."

I couldn't be sure because of all the blood, but I thought I observed a small flash of indignation in the bloodstained man's face. "I most certainly do know my own name."

"And that name is?"

"My name is Percy Lefroy. Two men attacked me as the train started travelling through the Merstham tunnels."

I remained silent, knowing that Holmes was far more skilled in asking questions about crimes than I was.

"Very well, Mr. Lefroy. Did you know your assailants?"

"No, they were strangers to me."

"Can you describe them?"

"Well… no, not really. They moved so quickly, I couldn't get a proper look at them. I remember that they were unusually tall and strong, though."

"You have no recollection of their hair or eye color? Their clothing? Did they have facial hair?"

"I… couldn't tell you. I just can't remember. They just came up to me, beat me, robbed me… and the next thing I know I'm here, and I don't have a clue what's happened to me."

A constable's arrival interrupted the conversation, and the official representative of the law quickly took charge of the bloodstained man, hurrying him off to the police station to lodge a complaint before receiving a full medical examination.

I could tell from the glint in my friend's eye that he had no intention of taking the train back to London. He was far too intrigued by the grisly discovery, and once he was on the scent of a case, there was no stopping him.

"That poor fellow," I murmured.

"Poor? I wonder…"

"Well, surely he's the victim of a terrible crime."

"Nonsense! There's no "surely" about it, Watson. His story is deficient in so many ways, I'm surprised that he didn't blush with embarrassment at his own perfidy. Although, due to all of the blood covering him, it's quite possible that his face did turn crimson without our realizing it."

"Deficient? Whatever do you mean?"

"Surely, my dear fellow, you realized right away that the blood covering that man was not his own."

"Well, yes. That was clear after a brief examination."

"And I realized that after only a second's glance. After all, a man who had lost that much blood would be at death's door and would probably be unable to move. No, that wasn't his own blood. Now it's possible that he had somehow wandered into an abattoir, but

I am never one to embrace a comparatively innocent option when a far more sinister one will suffice. Judging by the spatter on the man we just met, it's entirely probable that the blood came from a particularly violent fight with another human being, and as noted earlier, the loss of that much blood means that the other party involved in the fight is more likely to be dead than alive. Now, you noticed no serious wounds on that blood-covered man. I submit, that when a man is attacked by another man with a weapon that can draw a large amount of blood, the innocent victim is highly likely to be seriously injured, even if that person does manage to turn the tables in the end. But this man sustained no injury, a condition more probable in an assailant than a victim."

"I agree with you that it's more probable, but not necessarily. Suppose he was attacked by a drunkard or a madman. The assailant could have swung a knife or some other weapon about wildly, but his impaired condition could have made it fairly easy for his would-be victim to have turned the tables."

"Possibly, possibly. But did you observe the watch-chain on the bloodstained man?"

I allowed myself to smile a bit. My observational skills have improved quite a bit over the last few months, and I'd noticed that there was no watch or chain in the bloodstained man's jacket or vest pockets when I examined him. I said as much, and my fleeting sense of triumph was crushed by my friend's superior grin.

"The bloodstained man's watch-chain wasn't in his jacket or vest, Watson. It was sticking out of his boot."

"Was it?"

"Yes, a little under an inch of it was visible coming out of the top of his right boot. Now, that is suggestive, is it not?"

"Well, I suppose it's odd, but I don't see how it could be considered suggestive."

"My dear fellow, why would a man shove his watch-chain into his boot? If he wished to consult his pocket watch, he would leave it in his jacket or vest. If it were damaged or if he'd lost his watch, he might conceivably keep the chain it in his overcoat pocket. Under what circumstances might he have placed his watch-chain in his boots?"

"Perhaps if he were trying to protect it from being stolen? If he feared a pickpocket or an armed robber, he might have hidden the watch-chain there in the hopes that no one would look there."

"That is certainly within the realm of possibility, I agree with you. But you're missing a critical point. If an innocent man were taking care to protect his watch-chain, he would make quite certain it was completely hidden inside his boot. And if a man was attacked by a drunken madman, like you suggested, then he would have no time to secrete his watch-chain into a hiding place. A sudden attack would provide him with no opportunity to do so, and as we just discussed a few moments ago, an unexpected attack is by far the most likely way an innocent man might have escaped an assault unscathed. Therefore, the postulation that the watch-chain was hidden in the boot as a precaution will simply not hold water."

"Then why would the watch-chain be in his boot? Are you saying that he tucked away his own watch-chain to bolster his claim that he'd been robbed?"

"I very much suspect that the watch-chain in question doesn't actually belong to him, but to his victim. An intelligent criminal would have accepted the loss and disposed of the watch-chain, and if the chain truly belonged to him, he would have sold or pawned it if he were in dire need of money. It's more likely that he stole the watch-chain, and then hid it in his boot so that he would not have committed his crime for nothing. Being in a hurry to hid his ill-gotten gains, he neglected to conceal the chain completely."

"Then this man isn't an innocent victim of a crime, but a perpetrator."

"That is a reasonable theory at present. I shall need to investigate further in order to verify my theories."

"Will you tell the police to arrest him, Holmes?"

"No point in that, I regret to say. We have no solid evidence that will justify an arrest. I need to collect some more clues before I can make a proper charge. If I were to go about accusing men of committing murders with no corpses, even if I were entirely correct it's likely that I would wind up in court facing a lawsuit for slander. Not my preferred use of time and funds, I can assure you. No, our investigation must commence, and quickly, before our gory friend vanishes. After he makes his statement to the police and cleans himself up, there's nothing to keep him here."

"Then what is our next step?"

"If you'll follow me, Watson, I want to take a look at the train currently waiting at the station. I daresay we shall find some useful information there."

And with that, Holmes led the way to the train and climbed aboard. He worked his way down the train car, glancing into each room of the carriage, until he finally scrutinized one door handle more closely.

"Aha! Here we are, Watson! This is the one we want."

"How can you tell?"

"The smears of blood on the handle, of course. The dark color of the door handle makes them difficult for the untrained eye to see– the casual observer may mistake them for rust. I, however, have made a special study of how blood responds to various surfaces. I have started a very promising monograph that I really must finish some day on how bloodstains appear on various kinds of wood and metals. These little marks that could easily pass for rust? They have a far more sinister meaning, I assure you."

With that, Holmes withdrew a handkerchief from his pocket and gingerly opened the door. He took a very swift look around, and turned back to me.

"This is the scene of the crime, no doubt about that."

"Are you sure?"

"My dear Watson, the copious amounts of blood on most of the surfaces, the damage to the room indicating a struggle, the abandoned, bloodstained personal items, and the three bullet holes in the wall all lead to the unescapable conclusion that a violent crime has been committed here. It is beyond the bounds of probability to suppose that two particularly sanguineous attacks have taken place in the same train car within the past hour. The dampness of the larger patches of blood and the lingering scent of gunpowder prove the recentness of the violence that occurred here."

"Shall we speak to the police and have him arrested now?"

"Of course not. We need to find the real victim of this case. But we will go straight to the authorities and tell them of our discovery."

We could have made it to the police station in less than five minutes, but we had the unfortunate poor luck to be confronted by a pair of train conductors who had wandered into the carriage, spotted the two of us amongst all of the carnage, and drew the erroneous conclusion that we were responsible for the mess. We tried to explain the situation to them, but the dim-witted pair were holding fast to their first impression, and they blew their whistles and summoned the police. Seeing as how they were disposed to make trouble if we attempted to flee, Holmes explained to me that we might as well stand and wait, and we ought to be able to explain away the situation in a matter of minutes.

Holmes' prediction proved overly optimistic, and it took nearly an hour to convince the local constabulary that we had only been investigating a crime. It was only Holmes' repeated pointing out of the facts that neither of us had any wounds upon us that could have caused the bloodshed, that neither of us were carrying a firearm, and that the state of the blood's coagulation indicated that whatever had happened there had taken place sometime earlier, that the police reluctantly but wholeheartedly conceded that we had nothing to do with the carnage. Furthermore, the realization that this was the scene of the crime that had led to that mysterious man getting covered in blood had a galvanizing effect on the Chief Constable in charge of the case.

"Well, I thank you for bringing the possible murder scene to our attention, Mr. Holmes," the Chief Constable told us with a moderate amount of grace. "But we would've found it fairly quickly on our own, I'm sure you know that. And thank you for those very insightful theories about the case as well."

"Will you be holding that man?" I asked.

"I don't think we can, sir. We've interviewed him, and I must say I've had my suspicions of him from the start. We policemen aren't fools, you know. You weren't here when Mr. Lefroy made his statement, but I noticed a fair number of holes in his story, though I did suppose we might be able to chalk them up to mental distress over the incident. It could affect anybody's memory, don't you know."

"Where is Mr. Lefroy now?" Holmes inquired.

"I suppose he's at the hospital. They're giving him a full examination, and we'll see what he has to say for himself after a bit of rest and time to collect his thoughts."

"May we speak to him?"

"You'd have to check with his doctors. If the man's in a state of shock like one of the doctors suspected, they might not allow anybody to question him."

Holmes craned his neck and examined a small cardboard box on the Chief Constable's desk. "Are these Mr. Lefroy's possessions?" he asked, pointing at the label.

"They are. Care to examine them?"

"I would. Holmes picked up a pair of golden coins and held them up, one in each hand.

"Now, why would a man be desperate enough to rob someone else when he had a couple of sovereigns in his pocket?" the Chief Constable mused.

"Oh, these aren't sovereigns," Holmes replied, tossing them on the desk, where they made a dull clunking noise. He withdrew a pocket knife from his coat and scratched the face of both coins, leaving a dark scrape on them. "Gilded lead. These sovereigns are counterfeit."

There was silence for several moments, and I broke it. "At the very least, are you going to arrest him for possessing counterfeit coins?"

The Chief Constable did not respond, and eventually Holmes responded, "It would be very difficult to make a passable case out of that, Watson. After all, we have no proof that Mr. Lefroy actually knew that these sovereigns were not genuine coin of the realm. All he has to do is claim that he was unknowingly given these coins by a bank or business and that is enough to shed a reasonable doubt upon his guilt. In any case, why arrest him for a trifling crime when a much greater crime, possibly mere assault but more likely murder, has been committed?"

"Are you proposing a course of action, Mr. Holmes?" The Chief Constable seemed oddly willing to listen to a non-policeman's ideas for continuing the investigation.

Holmes nodded. "I am. Where is Lefroy?"

"I just got a message from one of my men telling me that the hospital's given him a clean bill of health and that he's on his way to board the next train to London."

"Surely that shows a guilty conscience," Holmes mused. "The man wants to flee as soon as possible. Additionally, he's not bothering to pick up the so-called sovereigns. That's highly indicative that he knows they're counterfeit, and doesn't want to return to the police station to retrieve them. When does that train leave?"

"In just under nine minutes. Perhaps a bit less– my watch runs slow."

Holmes turned to me. "Watson! Hurry to the train station, purchase a ticket to London, find Lefroy, and ride back with him. Don't let him out of your sight. And be on your guard. I believe he's already seriously harmed one man today, I certainly do not want you to be the second. Meanwhile, Chief Constable, will you kindly allow me to assist your men with a search of the line?"

I followed my orders to the letter, and I managed to board the train moments before it pulled away from the station. The train was not particularly crowded, so it was an easy matter to come across Lefroy. He was wearing a clean suit, but it was one of the old, worn, third-hand pieces that hospitals often keep on hand for the indigent. It did not fit him well, and the legs of his trousers were considerably longer than necessary, so the tops of his boots were completely covered and it was impossible for me to tell if he still had the watch-chain hidden inside one.

I maneuvered myself into a seat one row behind and across the aisle from Lefroy, who was slouched down and staring at his boots. My mind raced as I attempted to figure out what the best course of action would be. Did I introduce myself to him? Should I try to strike up a conversation? Twice, my mouth opened in order to speak to him, but a moment's thought led me to clamp my lips closed again, figuring that perhaps it was best to keep my presence a secret. After all, what if he remembered me from the train station? No, it was surely a more prudent course of action to try to follow him unobserved.

The train ride was uneventful, and one station before we reached London, a grubby-faced young boy poked me in the elbow. "This is for you, Doctor." He pushed a telegram into my hand. "Mr. Holmes said you'd have half a crown for me."

I thought it presumptuous of Holmes to dole out my half-crowns without my permission, but I figured that he and I could settle accounts when we met again. As I dropped the coin into the boy's hand, I wondered how he'd gotten aboard the train, but he turned around and vanished before I could ask him the question.

Opening the telegram, I read the message:

WATSON–

BODY FOUND. DON'T LET LEFROY OUT OF YOUR SIGHT. WHEN YOU DO LOSE TRACK OF HIM, WIRE ME IMMEDIATELY.

HOLMES

My first reaction upon reading this telegram was indignation. Holmes has developed a frustrating habit of assuming the worst about my abilities, and the fact that he is often more correct than I'd like him to be is a continual source of irritation on my part. Still, though I had no real experience shadowing other people in the street without being detected, I noted that the sun had recently set, and a light London fog was drifting into the area. I reasoned that these new developments would help keep me hidden from my quarry, though I immediately realized that a tandem consequence of the darkness and fog was the fact that I would have increased difficulty keeping Lefroy in my sights.

I managed to keep an average of ten paces behind Lefroy over the next three blocks, but a throng of churchgoers exiting a small chapel blocked my line of sight, and by the time I made my way through the group of worshippers, I found that Lefroy was nowhere to be found. I hurried ahead in the hopes of catching up with him, but I felt my heart leap up so high it nearly hit my chin when a hand reached out of the alley and gripped my shoulder firmly.

"Who the hell are you and why are you following me?"

I found myself quite unable to speak, and as I turned around, I realized that the man holding on to my shoulder was Lefroy himself. My muteness proved no serious problem, as Lefroy recognized me immediately.

"Here now, didn't I see you at the station in Brighton?"

Mercifully, I regained control of my vocal chords. "Yes. I'm a doctor, you see. My name is Watson. The hospital was very concerned about you and wanted someone to keep an eye on you. Since I was on my way back home to London, anyway, I volunteered to follow you and make sure that you got home safely. I didn't introduce myself because I didn't want to disturb your quiet time to yourself, you see. After a terrible shock like the one that you endured this afternoon, it seems only right that you should be given as much space as possible in order to process everything."

I felt the overpowering desire to keep talking, but I realized that babbling would only serve to raise Lefroy's suspicions, and I forced myself to be silent.

Would he believe what I said? If he was the violent fiend that Holmes suspected him of being, might he attack me? I met Lefroy's gaze directly, and tried to make my eyes unsuspicious and unthreatening, hoping that he would view me as a well-meaning friend.

Lefroy's eyes remained focused on mine for what seemed like hours. His expression was hard and accusatory, but unexpectedly and instantaneously, it transformed, becoming relieved and amiable.

"Oh, I say. How very decent of you."

"Not at all, my dear fellow."

"I do appreciate your going to such lengths to look out for my wellbeing. But I don't want you to go to any trouble. I was just on my way to my relative's boarding-house where I've been staying." He fingered the shabby, ill-fitting suit he was wearing. "I need to change my clothes."

"I don't mind joining you if you don't mind my presence," I replied, trying to sound nonchalant. "It'd give me a clear conscience to make sure that you got home safely."

"All right, then, thank you! But you're in for a bit of a walk, I'm afraid. The boarding house is in the Wallington district."

That was indeed a bit of a trek for me, but I decided that despite my many purchases earlier that day, I could afford a small luxury. "I must insist that you let me pay for a carriage-ride."

He demurred, then agreed with minimal coaxing on my part. Soon afterwards, we arrived at the boarding house. He wished me good night and made his way into the building.

I abruptly realized that I was in a tricky situation. I didn't know if the boarding house had a back exit, and there was no convenient place for me to hide and observe unseen. There was no way that I could make sure Lefroy was resting in his room. I was fretting over the best course of action when a young street urchin jumped into the carriage with me.

"Who are you, young fellow?"

"My name's Cookney, Doctor. I just heard from Mr. Holmes, and I'm to give you this telegram."

I opened it, and read–

WATSON–

> VICTIM IDENTIFIED. ISSAC GOLD, FORMER CORN MERCHANT. BOTH GUNSHOT AND KNIFE WOUNDS. HAVE YOU LOST LEFROY YET? IF SO, RETURN TO 221B AND WAIT FOR ME.
>
> —

HOLMES

Once again, my initial response was indignation, but the abrupt realization that I did not, in fact, know for certain that Lefroy was securely in his room tempered my umbrage. After I hastily tossed the carriage driver his fee, I hurried into the boarding house, planning on making up some story about wishing to rent a room there, thereby giving me access to the building.

Before I could reach the door, I felt a faint tug at the back of my coat. Turning around, I saw Cookney.

"It's too late, Doctor. Didn't you hear the whistle?"

"What whistle?" I had been so lost in my thoughts, a cannon could've gone off without my noticing.

"A couple of my pals gave the signal. Mr. Holmes gave us all some special whistles a while back. If you're young– around our age– or if you have unusually sensitive ears like Mr. Holmes, you can hear them. Most adults can't. The whistles are very high-pitched. Anyway, Lefroy went out the window about two minutes after he entered the boarding house."

"We need to catch him!"

"Don't you worry, Doctor. My pals are right on his heels. About an hour ago, I got a message from Mr. Holmes to pick up this special preparation of his from his home."

"What special preparation?"

"Couldn't tell you for sure what was in it, but it smells like a mixture of anise and vanilla extract. Rather nice, really. Anyway, I snuck in through the coal chute, found Lefroy's room, and sprayed all the clothes and boots in his closet with the preparation. Mr. Holmes figured Lefroy would change his clothes and make his escape. But my pals are tracking him. Bobby'll catch him."

"You seem to have a lot of faith in that boy Bobby."

"Bobby's not a boy, he's a spaniel. Best nose in London. Wherever Lefroy goes, Bobby will follow the scent."

I stood silently for a moment, reflecting on both Holmes' ingenuity and his absolute confidence in a dog and a bunch of street urchins. "So what am I to do?"

"Just what the telegram said. Go back to 221B and wait. One of my pals is wiring Mr. Holmes."

"My carriage is probably long gone by now."

"No, I told the driver to wait. May I ride back with you?"

And so, a little over an hour later, I found myself back at 221B, eating one of Mrs. Hudson's hot dinners and wondering just where Lefroy was at that moment.

I was two bites away from finishing my meal when Holmes walked in the door.

"Ah, Watson! Enjoying your meal, I hope? I've asked Mrs. Hudson to send up my meal as well. You won't mind if I eat while I tell you the results of the last few hours, do you?"

"Not at all."

Mrs. Hudson entered and set down a large plate of stew with rolls in front of Holmes, who smiled and began enjoying it immediately.

I allowed Holmes some time to nourish himself, but after a few minutes my curiosity got the better of me and I practically begged him to provide me with some news on the case.

"Ah, yes. I must say, Watson, this case was a great disappointment to me. There was no artistry, no cleverness, no imagination. None of the hallmarks of the great criminal, or even an inspired miscreant. Simply a bare, bland case of brutality and greed, resulting in a wasted life. I tell you, this Lefroy, if that is his true name, which I very much doubt, has done nothing to distinguish himself as a criminal. Nothing more than a modern highwayman, who sacrificed another human being with every right to live for a pittance."

"There was a murder, then?"

"Yes, and it required no real effort of my intellectual powers to resolve the case. It was obvious from the very beginning that a violent crime occurred in that train compartment, and that no man could survive such a substantial loss of blood. That left the question of what happened to the body, and I suspected that the killer had simply pushed it out the window, possibly in a place where it might not be spotted for quite some time. A tunnel might be a logical place for disposing of the body, where it could be jettisoned from the train in darkness and lie undiscovered for hours, even days.

After analyzing the state of the coagulation of the blood in the carriage, I had a fair idea of how much earlier the crime had occurred. I therefore subtracted the amount of time since the train arrived in the station, and after calculating the average speed of the train, determined that there was only one tunnel in the estimated range, and asked the police to check it.

There, they found a body that was quickly identified as one Isaac Gold, a gentleman of mature years who was now enjoying a comfortable retirement. An aged, rather frail man whose clothing illustrated his prosperous condition was a natural target for a marauder. The body suffered numerous bullet and knife wounds. His watch and chain had been ripped from his waistcoat, and all of his money was removed from his wallet and pockets. Poor fellow."

"And you think that Lefroy is the killer?"

"I'm quite sure of it, Watson. The motive was robbery, a crime of opportunity. It was just the late Mr. Gold's bad luck to have been the selected victim. It might have been any one of a hundred other people. Lefroy– or whatever his real name is– will not escape the grasp of justice for long. I have utter confidence that between my ragtag collection of street urchins, the keen nose of Bobby, and the efforts of the police, Lefroy will be arrested within a very short time, and will doubtless pay the ultimate price for his crimes."

Holmes' predictions proved completely accurate. Lefroy was swiftly arrested and charged with the crime. Holmes and I were among the prosecution witnesses at the trial, where it was revealed that Lefroy's true name was Mapleton, and that he'd attempted to rob the unfortunate Mr. Gold, but Gold's refusal to be cowed into compliance led to Lefroy– or rather Mapleton– to turn to lethal violence.

After the announcement of the guilty verdict, Holmes and I discussed the case back at our lodgings.

"A sad crime, but not without its points of interest," Holmes remarked.

"One point still bothers me, Holmes. Why was Lefroy– or rather, Mapleton– sitting down at the station when the ticket collector found him?"

"Most likely, he realized that he was covered in blood and realized that he couldn't get away without attracting attention. So he decided to collapse and act as if he'd been injured in order to deflect suspicion.?"

"That makes sense," I replied. "You know, I can't say that I came across very well in this case. I let him escape out from under my nose."

"You're new to the field of catching criminals, my dear fellow. Give yourself a bit more time and experience. And indeed, if you wish to write up this case, you can always utilize a touch of artistic license to make your role a bit more heroic."

"Thank you for your generosity of spirit, Holmes, but I think that if I do choose to record this case for posterity, I shall adhere strictly to the truth. Accuracy is very important to me."

Holmes laughed. "If only the newspapers were as scrupulous as you, Watson."

"What do you mean?"

Holmes withdrew the evening edition of a newspaper from his pocket and dropped it on the table. "Read the coverage of our case, Watson."

I did so. When I reached the last paragraph, I read aloud, "The police are particularly indebted to the assistance of an independent detective, Mr. George Holmes... *George* Holmes! Wherever did they come up with that name? Who in their right minds could ever mistake the name "George" for "Sherlock?""

My friend smiled. "I have no idea, but I shall take this as a lesson. Never seek out fame in the popular press. Any attempt to catch the public eye is bound to have unintended consequences, especially when reporters have such difficulty keeping stories straight. No, I think that in the future, wherever possible I shall refrain from accepting any public acknowledgement of my role in solving crimes. Unless of course, you decide to record my exploits, Watson. You are the one person who I trust to get all of the details correct..."

Author's note: The murder of Isaac Gold was a true case from 1881, and the basic narrative and most of the characters, including the detective "George Holmes," are taken from history. The idea that the papers got Holmes' name wrong is of course, purely my own invention.

The Chapel of the Holy Blood

It is often said that two heads are better than one, although this is by no means a universally shared perspective. When an acquaintance once repeated this dictum to Father Brown, the priest immediately replied that when two heads of state get together, the result often leads to war. His acquaintance retreated immediately, and from that point forward was noticeably recalcitrant to engage the good Father in any form of conversation whatsoever. Father Brown has never complained about that.

It was a dreary Thursday afternoon, and as the little priest was making his way down Baker Street, he was holding tightly to his umbrella. The weather was so blustery that had anybody bothered to look at Father Brown, they would have worried that a sudden gust of wind would send the priest flying over London. No one was seriously concerned about his welfare, however, as everybody on the street that day was completely engrossed in their own affairs, and there was so little light that a small man clad all in black and covering himself with a black umbrella was virtually invisible.

When Father Brown knocked on the door of 221B, Mrs. Hudson informed him that Sherlock Holmes was currently out and she didn't know when he'd be back, but he was more than welcome to wait in his rooms. Father Brown stood by the fire, waiting for his cassock to dry, and sustained himself with the pot of tea and the plate of Scottish shortbread that Mrs. Hudson had thoughtfully provided for him.

After about twenty minutes, the priest was shaken out of his daydreaming when a familiar voice called out to him. "My dear Father Brown! How wonderful to see you!"

"Holmes! I hope that I haven't arrived at an inconvenient time."

"Not at all. I just resolved a rather disappointing situation involving a banker absconding with funds. His initial trick of using mirrors to make it appear that the vault he'd been pilfering from was fuller than it was had at least a touch of ingeniousness to it, but his getaway plan was shamefully obvious. His disguise was positively laughable. In any case, he is now sitting uncomfortably in jail and the stolen funds have been recovered. I shall not go into any more detail. The crime simply is not that interesting. Anyway, how are you, Father? I haven't seen you since we solved the case of the two Coptic Patriarchs together."

"I'm quite well, thank you. I've been working at the Deaf School along with my usual parish duties, and my old friend Flambeau is coming for a visit next week."

"Good old Flambeau! Give him my best, will you?" Holmes had met the reformed thief Flambeau a few years earlier during the case of the Vatican cameos. Flambeau had been the chief suspect, and Holmes and Father Brown's combined efforts had managed to clear his name and prevent an international uproar.

"Where is Doctor Watson?"

"He's at a conference in Wales now. Won't be back for several hours. He'll be sorry to have missed you."

"And I'm disappointed to have missed him this visit."

The two men helped themselves to tea and shortbread. Father Brown checked his cassock and after he assured himself that it was dry, he settled down in a chair next to Holmes.

"So Father, what brings you all the way to London on this most inclement day?"

"I came to you because I needed your assistance– particularly your knowledge of chemistry."

"Indeed? Is there a matter of science that you needed to discuss?"

"There is. If it isn't too much trouble, I need you to use your famous re-agent."

"The one precipitated by haemoglobin?"

"The very same." Father Brown reached into his pockets and pulled out a rosary, a breviary, four small coins, a whistle, a compass, two sticks of chocolate, and three handkerchiefs (all of different colors) before finally pulling out a small glass jar containing traces of a dried reddish substance.

"Is that blood, Father?"

"I was hoping that you could tell me whether it is or not."

Holmes' face lit up, and he happily snatched the jar from Father Brown's hands and rushed over to his small laboratory. "I shall fill this flask with water, and I just need to take a tiny bit of this sample– as much that will cover the tip of this bodkin here. Now just one moment…" Holmes shook the flask vigorously, dropped some pale crystals into the solution, and then uncorked a bottle full of clear liquid and shook a tiny trickle of it into the flask. After about four seconds the water turned the color of strong tea.

"Is that a positive test, Holmes?"

"Well, yes… and no. The haemoglobin test is positive, but… the color of the test result isn't quite right. It isn't dark enough. Which means…" Holmes drew another tiny sample from the jar, spread it onto a glass slide, and slid it onto his microscope. "If I'm right, the red blood cells will be slightly oval… Yes, by thunder, they are!"

Father Brown's face brightened. "That means that's not human blood, then?"

"I'm afraid I can't be positive, but based on my previous experiments with animal blood like beef and chicken, I'd be willing to give fair odds that this blood came from a sheep."

"That's better. That's very much better." Father Brown smiled, walked back to his chair, and sat.

"Are you at liberty to explain where the blood came from, Father?"

"Oh, yes. The seal of the confessional is not a factor here." Leaning forward, Father Brown turned to Flambeau, who had returned to the chair next to him. "Have you ever heard of Dirus Castle?"

"I dare say I may have come across its name in the newspapers at some point, but at present I can recall nothing about it."

"Dirus Castle was for many centuries a monastery. When Henry VIII seized most of the Catholic Church's property for his own use and gave much of what was left to his powerful friends, he sent a squadron of armed men to seize the monastery, which was located on some particularly fertile farmland. The monks were known for beekeeping and other agrarian pursuits, but they were not trained fighters, and in a very short time all of the monks were slaughtered.

What happened next is obscured by legend. According to the story my niece told me, the abbot was the last to be slain, but as he was dying from a mortal blow, he placed a curse on the property, claiming that every so often, the blood of the slain monks would trickle down the halls of the monastery as a reminder of this horrific crime."

Holmes arched an eyebrow. "Do you– er– believe that story, Father?"

"Oh, I'm quite convinced of the veracity of the first bit of the tale– the part where Henry VIII ordered the murder of a lot of members of the clergy and stole their land. That's well-documented, despite the current owners' attempts to hush up the violent history behind what's now called Dirus Castle. You see, the title of Lord Dirus was bestowed upon a particularly brutal fellow who raised a great deal of money and land for Henry VIII and his allies by killing anybody who opposed the King and seizing everything of value. I may say, Lord and Lady Dirus don't like people knowing that the family lands, funds, and titles derive from a massacre of unarmed monks. They prefer everybody to think that their titles derive from antiquity, and that the family's lineage dates back to the Knights of the Round Table. All tosh, of course."

"But what do you think about the curse, Father?"

The priest smiled. "I suppose that given my personal predilections, I'd prefer to think that a dying man of the cloth would choose to spend his dying moments praying for the souls of those who persecuted him rather than using his last breath calling for vengeance through sanguineous haunting. I certainly believe in miracles and the supernatural, but I can also smell a rat. And I believe that some sort of fakery is happening at Dirus Castle at the moment. You see, Holmes, I took that sample of blood from the walls of the castle."

"Are you saying that there really was blood flowing from the walls?"

"Well, not really flowing. Earlier this morning, trickles of a dark reddish substance, presumably blood, were found smeared and splattered all over the walls. I took this sample from the inside of Lord Dirus' study, which was once a room of private contemplation for the monastery known as, ironically enough, the Chapel of the Holy Blood."

"Did Lord or Lady Dirus call you in to investigate, Father?"

"Oh dear me, no. The Dirus family is decidedly antireligious. They have nothing but cold hostility for me and everybody of my faith and vocation. But my niece, Betty, is engaged to the son of Lord and Lady Dirus. A young fellow named Agro."

"Best wishes to her. What is this Agro like?"

"Holmes, I believe that in Doctor Watson's account of "The Copper Beeches" that you discussed how the character of parents can be seen in their children, and vice versa."

"I did. In the case that you refer to, I was talking about a particularly nasty and cruel boy, and I postulated that he inherited his unpleasant demeanor from one or both of his parents. Am I right in thinking that your niece's fiancé is... not such a pleasing youth as you'd hope?"

The priest made a face. Even though he couldn't see his own expression, he was quite sure that anybody watching him might conceivably concluded that he was being uncharitable. Anybody familiar with young Agro would have found Father Brown's reaction understated. Dozens of the family's former servants had surreptitiously warned away potential employees with horror stories of the tantrums that the heir to the title was prone to throwing.

Holmes smiled, "My dear Father Brown, you needn't worry about speaking ill of others. It so happens that on a recent case I interviewed a kitchen maid, and though she could provide very little in the way of information useful to my investigation, she told me a great deal about her previous employer. Lord Dirus is an angry man, a womanizer, and excessively fond of the bottle. His son follows in his footsteps, and Lady Dirus is a coldhearted, imperious woman who doesn't just work her staff to the bone, but to the marrow as well."

Taking a sip of tea, Holmes redirected the topic. "How, exactly, did your niece become engaged to that fellow? If your niece's character bears any resemblance to your own, then I doubt that Betty and Agro are compatible."

"They are not."

"Will you take offense to my broaching the possibility that your niece may be... shall we say... blinded by the glamour of lands and a title?"

"Oh, no. Betty is not a golddigger. Her mother, however, has always wanted her daughter to marry "well," and Betty has always tried to appease her mother at all times. In any case, Betty has had bad luck with previous suitors. More than one of these seemingly respectable young men has proven to be a criminal, and the cycle has been going on for rather a long time. Betty has, unfortunately, developed a certain amount of anxiety about her unmarried state, and I believe that she has latched onto this relationship both to please her mother and because she has come to the deeply flawed conclusion that a bad marriage is better than no marriage at all."

"Father, have you come to me for help in breaking up this engagement?"

"No, though that would be a welcome development. I visited you today in the hopes that your test would confirm whether or not the substance on the walls of the chapel was blood or not, and if so, if that blood was human. Depending on your verdict, I was going to investigate further in the hopes of explaining why the blood was decorating the castle walls."

A delighted look spread across Holmes' face. "Would it be presumptuous if I were to offer my services?"

Father Brown immediately accepted Holmes' offer, and half an hour later the pair were on a train bound for Dirus Castle. Once the train was on its way, Holmes asked, "Explain again to me what you observed this morning, please."

"My niece invited me to elevenses at the castle, and I met her in the village and walked with her to visit her intended and his family. When we arrived, we could see at once that there were bloodstains on part of the wall of the entryway. Young Agro showed us into his father's similarly-stained study on one side of the entryway, which used to be the Chapel of the Holy Blood when the structure was a monastery, and rather gleefully told us about the legend– which I was already familiar with– and declared that the abbot's curse was at work."

"Interesting. You say that Agro seemed happy about the blood on the walls. Has he ever, to your knowledge, showed any interest in the supernatural?"

"On the contrary, as I said earlier, Holmes, the family has a reputation for being particularly antireligious. When Agro waxed lyrical about the abbot's curse and the vengeance of the slaughtered monks, his parents were standing there, gritting their teeth and glaring at Betty and myself. Neither of them had anything to say about the blood on the walls. Indeed, they wanted to ignore it altogether."

"Really?" Holmes pressed his fingertips together underneath his chin. "You would think that they would have at least been interested in talking about it. After all, such an occurrence mustn't happen every day. It would have made for some amusing conversation over elevenses."

"I agree with you. Unfortunately, our meeting was particularly unpleasant. Lord Dirus and his son made a few derogatory remarks towards my profession and my religion, and when I contradicted them and defended my faith and vocation, they both became rather annoyed and left the room. As for Lady Dirus, she never said a word to me or to Betty, despite our best efforts to ask her questions about the phenomenon going on in her home."

Holmes permitted himself the faintest trace of a grin. "Far be it from me to criticize a lady, but I rather doubt that Lady Dirus is living up to the highest standards of hostessing. I am surprised that she didn't provide her future daughter-in-law with a warmer reception. Am I correct in theorizing that Lady Dirus is opposed to the match?"

"I should say that assessment is accurate. Betty comes a line of country squires that are rich in family history but poor in funds. I don't know the exact state of the Dirus finances, but people with substantial estates seem to be in constant need of more money to pay for the upkeep of their considerable property. In any case, they've shut up most of the castle to save on maintenance expenses. They're only using a tiny portion of the property, which is why we had our elevenses in the little dining nook right next to the chapel."

"And the landed classes of England realized a long time ago that the best and most reliable way of raising enough money to support one's estates is to marry money." Holmes' eyes glinted with amusement. "I've heard it said that when England's gentry with country estates start their families, they pray for a son to inherit the property, and they pray for a wealthy heiress for their son to marry about two decades down the line. I trust that you will take absolutely no offense when I ask, why exactly did young Agro agree to the match?"

"I regretfully but relievedly concluded a while ago that Betty was not entering into a love match. Agro is close to his parents, but one of his chief joys in life is riling them. I've made some enquiries, though I suppose that it would be ingenuous to call my questioning discreet. Apparently Agro likes to toy with his parents' nerves, and he has a reputation for courting attractive young women without a bean to their names, even getting engaged to them if it suits his fancy. Of course, none of these relationships ever come to anything."

"Wouldn't such behavior leave that pleasing youth vulnerable to the prospect of a breach of promise lawsuit? I know of at least two dozen cases where a wealthy young man has gotten engaged to a wholly unsuitable woman, and when he tries to extricate himself from the relationship, the young woman takes legal action over being jilted, and invariably receives an impressively lucrative settlement without ever having to enter a courtroom."

Father Brown sighed. "I suppose the financial risk is part of the sport for our friend Agro. When he tires of his latest lady friend, he engages in such boorish behavior that the young woman terminates the engagement. He's careful to have a friend of his as a witness at all times. That leaves him well immunized against any lawsuits. Indeed, my sources– most of them former employees of the Dirus family– make it clear that the girl is usually so relieved to be free from that singularly unpleasant young man that she would be willing to hand over her life's savings to her ex-fiancé if it meant that she would never have to see him again."

"I see. Do you think that your niece wants to escape from the relationship?"

"She hasn't said so in so many words, but if past patterns hold, the only reason why she entered the relationship in the first place was to please her mother. She's a very dutiful daughter, although perhaps it's a lot easier for her to pursue relationships with men she doesn't particularly care for than it is for her to listen to her mother complain about her marital status."

Holmes took a breath and redirected the conversation. "How exactly did you get that blood sample? Even if Lady Dirus wasn't speaking to you, I can hardly imagine that she would let you scrape off a bit of coagulated blood without protest."

"Lady Dirus walked away without so much as an "excuse me" when she finished her coffee. She did pause to give a large golden candelabra a quick dusting with her handkerchief before leaving the room. I went straight to the chapel– technically the current Lord Dirus' study, although I dare say that it was never officially decommissioned– and used the edge of a coin to remove a substantial amount of the blood. Luckily, I happened to have an old jam jar with me, though for the life of me I can't remember why I was carrying it with me in the first place. Betty was a bit nonplussed about the whole thing, but she was rather keen on the prospect of me coming to you. Betty's mother has gotten her into a number of excruciating relationships with unpleasant yet wealthy young men, but she's always been able to escape, usually with my help. Young Lord

Agro may be her least pleasant and most intimidating fiancé yet, and she was enthusiastic at the prospect of you getting involved in the situation, even if it was only to analyze the blood sample. In a situation like this, she wants as many allies as possible in her corner."

"Sensible young woman."

Holmes and Father Brown continued their discussion of the case for the rest of their journey. In a little under an hour, their train reached the tiny station on the outskirts of the village closest to Castle Dirus. At the priest's suggestion, they went directly to the Purple Boar, a pub where the former second footman at the Castle had found employment after an unpleasant incident involving an irate Lord Dirus and a tantrum involving a chamber pot and a flaming log from a fireplace.

"I tell you, I wouldn't go back to work at the Castle again, not if you paid me a million pounds. *Two* million," the ex-second footman declared as he poured drinks for Father Brown and Holmes. "They're batty, every last one of them. Lord Dirus is an absolute monster. When he's not drinking up half the wine cellar, he's chasing after girls from the village or the female staff. Not very dignified for a man of his age, is it? He's careful not to do anything untoward in the presence of his wife, of course. She's an iceberg, she is, but when somebody crosses her, that porcelain façade cracks pretty fast, if you get my drift. And the son takes after the father, you know. Chases after anything in a dress, and a fuse so short a single spark would burn it up completely in a half-second, it would. Why, I'll tell you about the time…"

The second footman turned publican continued expounding upon the many personal flaws and offensive aspects of the Dirus family, and Holmes and Father Brown sat and listened quietly, and marveled at the ease at which they were being provided with information on the local nobility's personal foibles. It was a full seven minutes before the former second footman took a breath, giving Holmes the chance to ask, "Do you happen to know how many members of the staff are left at the Castle?"

"Well, when I left last month, there were only four of us left. The housekeeper and both of the gardeners had given notice the week before, after Lord Dirus had gotten good and soused and fired his shotgun through the window at them– the gardeners, that is. And when the housekeeper ran into the room to see what had happened, he fired again at her! If I'd had any sense, I'd have left myself that day, especially considering how scant my wages were. They're not so well-off as they'd like us to think, you know. Lucky for me, I got out of there soon enough, and I found a place here. Not as fancy as the Castle, but a darned sight jollier."

"Who are the four remaining employees?" Holmes asked.

"Actually, only three now. A week after I made my happy escape, my pal, Lord Dirus' valet, decided he'd taken enough verbal abuse from the old… Better watch my language in front of a priest, I suppose. Anyway, he found a place working for a retired army colonel in the next village. Due to the Dirus family being short of ready cash, and the fact that their reputation for being terrible employers is well known for miles around, they haven't been replacing their missing staff members lately. The only ones left are that dotty old butler Bassett, who's half-senile but still manages to do his job. I think the only reason the butler sticks around is because he forgets Lord Dirus' insults the moment after he shouts them, and Lord Dirus keeps him around because his memory's so bad, Lord Dirus can claim he's already paid him his salary for the month, and the poor old fellow can't remember otherwise. Then there's the cook– a real tartar, that woman. The only staff member who can hold her ground against the members of the Dirus family. If she doesn't want to prepare something, she doesn't make it, even if the family demands it. Finally, there's Agnes, the housemaid. Pretty thing, though I'm disappointed to say that I've never gotten anywhere with her."

The former second footman continued to ramble for a long time after Father Brown and Holmes had finished their beverages. Most of what he told them was a rehash of what he'd previously said, although at times he would slip in the name of an unfortunate person, usually a maid or a girl from the village, whose life had been damaged

65

in some way due to coming into contact with the Dirus family. Eventually, the owner of the pub told the former second footman that he wasn't being paid to chat with the customers, and the mildly chagrined man turned to serving other customers.

As Father Brown and Holmes left the pub and walked through the village, Holmes turned to his friend and asked, "Do you remember the first case we investigated together?"

The priest nodded. "The sudden death of Cardinal Tosca. Of course."

"When we were following up on that note we found in the Cardinal's breviary, I told you that we needed to investigate the scene of the crime for clues. You told me that we needed to find out more about the Cardinal's character and what he truly believed him if we were ever going to find out why someone would want to kill him. In the end, we were both right. If we hadn't followed both lines of inquiry right away, we would never have proved it was murder or identified the culprit before it was too late and additional lives were lost."

"What are you saying, Holmes?"

"I mean, my friend, that we need to hurry up and investigate. Can you manage to get another invitation to Castle Dirus? If I can get a look at the bloodstains on the wall, and if you can try to gain some insight as to the family's behavior, I think that we can figure out what's going on here surprisingly quickly."

Father Brown explained that his niece had gone back to her mother in a nearby village, and that the Dirus family would never let him inside if they could help it, but that he was on friendly terms with the cook, and she would help them if they were to approach quietly by the servant's door.

When they arrived at the castle a quarter of an hour later, the cook was indeed happy to help them. Like nearly all of the other servants who had worked for the Dirus family, the cook made no pretense to any claims to loyalty to her unpleasant bosses.

Luck was on the side of the sleuths, and Father Brown and Holmes were able to make their way to the former chapel as stealthily as they possibly could without being seen by the other inhabitants of the castle. Upon reaching the chapel-turned-study, Holmes immediately whipped out a magnifying glass and began scrutinizing the bloodstains on the wall. Meanwhile, Father Brown crossed to the window, where he observed the three members of the Dirus family walking towards the house.

"Better hurry, Holmes. They're returning." After a moment the priest murmured, "I wouldn't have taken Agro for a gardener."

"What do you mean by that?" Holmes did not avert his eyes from the wall.

"He's carrying a shovel and a spade."

"Look at this, Father," Holmes pointed at the bloodstains. "Most of these droplets appear to be poured on the wall, as if someone took a bottle full of blood and gently tipped some of the contents down the sides. I don't think there's anything miraculous about this. Just a gory and unhygienic sight. However..." Holmes squinted. "Not all of these bloodstains follow the same pattern. I have made a study of the shapes blood droplets make during acts of violence. Most of the blood on these walls was gently poured. But here and there are different patterns of blood. Spattered droplets, rather like–"

Holmes was interrupted by the sound of the door clanging, and three pairs of feet came clamping towards the chapel.

"Well, that takes care of that," the gruff voice of Lord Dirus declared. "First thing tomorrow, I'm going to call that fellow and ask him to make good on his boasting and fix up a sixteenth-century document for us. Bassett? Bass-ETT? BASSETT!" Lord Dirus bellowed. "Get down here at once and make me a whiskey and soda. In the largest glass you can find, and don't feel it necessary to go heavy on the soda."

There was only one door to the former chapel, and nowhere to hide, not that Holmes and Father Brown had any intention of trying to avoid seeing the Dirus family. As father, mother, and son walked into the study, all three visibly blanched when they saw the two men standing there.

"Father Brown!" Agro blurted. "And... are you Sherlock Holmes?"

"What are you doing here?" Lady Dirus demanded.

"Investigating some very interesting bloodstains," Holmes replied smoothly. "I should like to speak to your housemaid, Agnes."

At this, all three members of the Dirus family swooned. Lady Dirus was the first to recover her composure. She clenched her jaw and pointed at Holmes and Father Brown. "You are not welcome here. Leave this instant or I shall summon the police and have you arrested for trespassing. And you will go to prison, whether you're a famous detective or a priest or not."

When asked about that moment later, Father Brown freely admitted that he had made an enormous leap, and that it would have served him right if he'd fallen flat on his face. Perhaps he was just lucky, and perhaps he had made a brilliant deduction based on meager evidence, but in any case, he came to the correct conclusion. "We'll be happy to leave, if you can produce your land grant to the Castle."

With that statement, Lord Dirus slumped to the floor, all the muscle strength seemed to have dissolved from Lady Dirus's shoulders, and young Agro crossed to the nearest decanter, tossed the stopper over his shoulder, and downed most of the contents with an enormous gulp. "What... what do you mean?" the no longer imperious Lady Dirus quavered.

"I mean, *Mrs*. Dirus," Father Brown put special stress on the title. "That I should like to see the documents that prove your ownership of this building, and your claims to nobility as well."

It is not necessary to describe the next five minutes in detail. Both Lord Dirus and Agro attempted to attack Holmes and Father Brown, but Holmes' knowledge of baritsu helped him to subdue both men. Lady Dirus lunged for Father Brown's throat, but luckily for the priest, the cook heard the commotion and hurried up to the chapel, holding a cast iron frying pan. When the cook saw Lady Dirus attempting to choke Father Brown, the tough but good-natured domestic had realized first, that she didn't care for Lady Dirus, second, that she did like Father Brown, third, that with her cooking skills she could find a better job elsewhere, and fourth, that she was holding a very heavy, blunt object.

One does not need to be a great detective to deduce what happened next.

Later that evening, after all three members of the Dirus family had been arrested, and Holmes and Father Brown were back in London, they told their story to a recently returned Watson.

"But surely an accusation of murder based on such little evidence was rather foolhardy, even for you, Holmes?" Watson remarked.

"I suppose it was, but based on the available clues, it was worth the risk in order to bring the perpetrators to justice. In any event, the nerves of that unholy family were already so badly frayed that it only took a very small tug to lead them to unravel altogether."

"Could the two of you please explain your thought processes from the beginning?"

"Of course, Watson. First of all, there was the issue of the blood on the walls of the former chapel. Let us assume that this is not some supernatural event based on a centuries-old curse– indeed, as Father Brown suspects, the narrative we have been told about the curse of the abbot is very likely highly fictionalized. If so, then why would blood be poured on the walls, blood that was probably that of a sheep, rather than human? The Dirus family would not willingly embrace such a sanguineous form of interior decoration, and it didn't appear to be a practical joke or a threat. If anything, according to Father Brown's narrative, they all seemed airily dismissive of the bloodstains and wanted us to ignore them. This odd behavior indicated that the blood caused no distress for them and did not interest them. Yet why wouldn't they want to make use of such a unique and effective conversation starter? Why did the notoriously irreverent Agro draw attention to the blood and then drop the subject?"

Holmes paused for effect and continued. "I must admit that I was at a loss until I examined the walls and discovered that there were two different patterns to the blood. There was the dribbled blood, and there was another set of stains that resembled a cast-off pattern, perhaps caused by the arterial spray that results when a person sustains a serious wound. In a moment, I realized the true purpose of the dribbled blood. It was meant to cover up blood that fallen on the wall in a violent attack, and from the amount of blood I saw that did not follow the dribbling pattern, the assault was most likely fatal."

"So far, so good," Holmes said after another dramatic pause. "But if there was an attack, there must be a victim. Who could it be? All three members of the Dirus family were accounted for, and they rarely hosted guests. Of course, the possibility of an intruder could not be dismissed, but what of the servants? We made inquiries and learned that at the moment, there were only three servants at the castle. We met the cook, she was unharmed. We heard Lord Dirus calling out to the butler, so we could eliminate him as a potential victim. That left the housemaid, Agnes. She was nowhere to be found, so she was the most likely victim. I formed a theory. The housemaid Agnes had been murdered. Perhaps she was having an affair with the notoriously lecherous Lord Dirus and Lady Dirus had bludgeoned her out of jealousy?"

"Wait a minute," Watson interjected. "How did you deduce that Lady Dirus was the killer? And that the death had been caused by bludgeoning?"

"Father Brown, why don't you expound on that point?" Holmes asked.

"Well, I formed a theory about what happened when I saw Lady Dirus polishing a candelabra with her handkerchief," the priest explained. "That's not the sort of thing that a noblewoman with a very high opinion of her own self-importance does of her own volition. She calls the maid and orders her to do a better job of cleaning. She doesn't lower herself to do a servant's work for her. That put two ideas into my head. First, that there was something on the candelabra that needed to be cleaned up right away and Lady Dirus couldn't wait for someone else to do it, and second, that either the maid wasn't to be trusted with this cleaning job, or more likely, that the maid wasn't around to do it."

"Father Brown and I had independently come to the same conclusions," Holmes continued. "For some reason, Lady Dirus had bludgeoned Agnes the housemaid with a candelabra, and her husband and son had helped her cover up the crime. The precise motive we'll address in a moment. I suspect it was young Agro who came up with the idea to take some sheep's blood– the cook was planning to make some mutton blood pudding that evening, so Agro probably crept downstairs and stole the bottle of sheep's blood from the larder. His mother's attack on poor Agnes led to stains on the wall, so what to do? They didn't have a maid to clean them up anymore. In any case, it's a time-consuming process to scrub blood out of the kind of absorbent stone used to build that part of the castle. With Father Brown and his niece coming soon, there was no time to clean it. Only one thing to do– spill a little sheep's blood to cover it all up. Father Brown just happened to take a sample from the sheep blood part by chance, though he could have easily taken some from the human blood portion, or some of both."

"But what was the motive?" Watson asked. "Are you saying that it wasn't jealousy over Agnes' affair with Lord Dirus?"

"Oh, no," Father Brown explained. "Lady Dirus was quite used to her husband's adultery, and in any case, she was sufficiently dispassionate towards her husband that any feelings of jealousy would have been completely impossible. Indeed, I don't think Agnes had an affair with Lord Dirus at all. No, there had to be another reason, only I never would have thought of it if I hadn't heard Lord Dirus talking about finding a forger to create a sixteenth-century document. I knew the history of how the family gained control of the castle through massacring a monastery, and everybody assumed that Henry VIII had given them the title and property through a royal land grant and decree. But what if for whatever reason, that never happened? If the King never signed an official document, then the Dirus family have no legal right to the castle, and they're not even really titled nobility. They've just occupied the property for centuries and called themselves "Lord" and "Lady," when in fact they're just squatters with pretensions of grandeur. I suppose that it's been a dark family secret generations, and somehow, poor Agnes came across some document or journal or something that revealed the truth while she was cleaning up and peeking through Lord Dirus's papers. And she realized that Lord and Lady Dirus were just "Mr. and Mrs. Dirus," and when for whatever reason she confronted them… Well, you know the rest. Holmes and I caught them returning from burying the body, which they'd hidden somewhere while they were waiting for my niece and I to leave. The police found poor Agnes in the woods after only a few minutes of searching."

After a long period of quiet, Watson asked, "What will happen to the castle? Will it be returned to the Church and become a monastery again?"

"Unlikely," Father Brown sighed. "That would require the British government admitting that most of the Church of England's property and much of the aristocracy's lands came from murder, theft, and centuries of denial. More likely, the powers that be in the government will find some loyal Member of Parliament who they think deserves a promotion, and they'll give him the estate and award him and his descendants some nice, impressive-sounding title."

The three men sat in silence for a moment.

"It seems your niece's engagement is at an end," Holmes remarked to the priest.

"And a good thing, too," Father Brown replied.

The Adventure of the Specious Spouse

"Will your wife be joining you tonight, Mr. Holmes?"

I was standing several feet behind Holmes, so I could not see the expression on his face. I did, however, observe his back stiffening and his hands clenching very slightly at the question posed by the maître d'.

"I am not married, sir. I will be dining with my colleague Dr. Watson tonight."

The maître d's eyebrows knotted. "Are you sure, sir?"

"Young man, I freely admit that I am not so young as I used to be. The Great War has taken its toll on all of us. Yet while the years may have passed, I can assure you that I am not completely senile. I am fully aware that I have never been married."

"I was certain that you were, Mr. Holmes."

"Are you a regular reader of my colleague's accounts of my cases? I am aware that, among the collection of individuals who enjoy his work, there is a subset who are convinced that I have been carrying on a relationship with one Irene Adler, but I can assure you that there is absolutely no truth to that rumor."

"Oh, not Miss Adler, sir, though I must say that I have wondered about her and you. No, I'm referring to Mary Grace Quackenbos Humiston. They call her 'Mrs. Sherlock Holmes,' you know, and seeing as how you've come all the way to New York City, sir, I thought that you were here to spend time with the missus."

Holmes's back stiffened even more. "I have never heard of this Mary Grace Quackenbos Humiston, and therefore there is no relationship between us. Will you show us to our table, please?"

"Of course, sir. Right away. I meant no offense, sir."

With a slight grunt of acknowledgement, Holmes followed the maître d' to a table in the far corner of the restaurant, and I was close behind them. After sending the maître d' on his way with a curt nod, Holmes and I picked up the menus.

"Does anything look particularly appetizing to you, Watson?"

"Aren't we going to discuss what just happened?"

"I fail to see any reason why I should upset myself shortly before eating. We came here to celebrate resolving a particularly sticky diplomatic situation between the United States, Great Britain, and Canada. I will not spoil my dinner by dwelling on a restaurant employee's comments."

I was about to speak, but I decided to hold my tongue. Holmes seemed to be in an uncharacteristically sour temper, and I did not wish to upset him further. Upon completing my second read-through of the menu, a realization struck me, and I was unable to stop myself from blurting out, "This isn't the first time that someone has asked you about being married to that woman, is it?"

Fortunately, Holmes did not appear to be annoyed at me for asking that question. "No, just the first instance of such inquiries being made in your presence, Watson. Over the course of the last two days, I have been asked that question nine times by people from walks of life ranging from shoeshine boys to city councilmen, all of them congratulating me on my marriage to this Mrs. Mary Grace Quackenbos Humiston. Invariably, when I insist that this woman is not my wife, I am met with skepticism. As if I would marry a woman, and then disclaim any connection to her in public."

"Why do you think that people are so adamant that you are indeed married to this lady?"

"I can only suppose that their imaginations have latched onto this pairing. I have often noticed with great bemusement that many individuals become fixated with the romantic lives of people in the public eye, and they develop irrational attachments to the relationships of the famous. Consider how people obsess about the marriage of members of the Royal Family. I dare say that a number of people here in New York rather like the idea of a local woman marrying me. Perhaps they think that I shall leave London and take up residence here."

"There are a great deal of interesting crimes here in New York City."

"Most certainly there are, and I believe that there are several skilled detectives who already call this metropolis home who are more than capable of solving any mysteries that the local criminal classes have to offer."

"I've heard of this Mrs. Humiston, you know. There was a profile of her in a magazine I read a couple of days ago. Do you know anything about her?"

"Other than that a surprising number of people are sorely confused as to her marital status, nothing at all."

"She's a lawyer, I believe, one of the few females to hold such a job, and she makes a career out of helping the poor and downtrodden. There was an Italian woman who was convicted of killing a man, and she was condemned to die. Mrs. Humiston took the case, found a number of problems with this trial, argued it was self-defense, and eventually had the sentence reduced to seven or eight years. Then she exposed a couple of scandals regarding immigrants to the American South — who were being held as slaves in all but name

— and ruffled a lot of feathers trying to drum up popular opinion against the practice. Then there was a young girl who disappeared, and after the police failed to find her, Mrs. Humiston identified a likely culprit, and after some clever strategizing, found the missing girl's body on the suspect's property. That was when they started to call her 'Mrs. Sherlock Holmes.' "

"If the reports that you read are correct, then she sounds like a very impressive woman."

"Yes, I.... Good heavens, Holmes!"

"What is it?"

"There was a picture of Mrs. Humiston in the article I read. I believe that she's here now!" I gestured toward the entryway. A woman in her fifties, with a bun of mostly dark hair covered with a large hat, was walking toward us. She had a rather regal bearing, and her dress was long and black, aside from a couple of thin white stripes on the sleeves. She exchanged a few words with the maître d', and after he pointed at us, she gave him a little nod; though I could not be certain of it, it was very possible that she slipped a little money onto the podium he was standing behind before she walked toward us.

Holmes turned and watched her approach us. He rose to his feet, and for a fleeting second I wondered if he was going to hurry out of the restaurant, but a moment's reflection told me that Holmes would never run away from a woman, at least a lady that did not intend him any physical harm. When Mrs. Humiston arrived at our table, he gave her a little nod of greeting.

"Mrs. Humiston?"

"That is correct."

"Would you care to join us?"

I have no idea how successful I was in masking my surprise when I rose and pulled over a chair from a nearby empty table, but Mrs. Humiston said "hello" to me with evident warmth and graciousness before taking her seat.

"You know who I am then, Mr. Holmes?"

"Watson has just provided me with a brief overview of your career."

"I suppose you know my nickname."

"Unfortunately, yes."

"I dare say you aren't very pleased about it."

"Admittedly, when I first heard the moniker 'Mrs. Sherlock Holmes' I was a trifle peeved. My initial reaction was that someone was building a reputation off of my name and career."

"It was not I who came up with that nickname, Mr. Holmes."

"I was rather certain that was the truth of the matter. And now, you wish for my help on a case?"

After many years of acquaintance with Holmes, I know never to be surprised by any of Holmes's deductions. Mrs. Humiston was not so used to Holmes's powers of observation. For a moment, I was afraid that she might fall back in her chair, but thankfully — even before I could reach to catch her — she regained her balance and gripped the table. "How did you know I needed your assistance, Mr. Holmes?"

"Why does anybody want to speak to me? You clearly have been trying to track me down, seeing as how you found me at this restaurant. I would not be surprised if you had allies or employees trying to find me."

"Mr. Julius Kron is a private detective who has worked with me on many occasions. He and a few assistants have spent the last day trying to track down the two of you. I heard from a mutual acquaintance that you were in town, and I realized that you might be able to help me. As soon as Mr. Kron informed me of your reservation at this restaurant, I decided to seize this opportunity."

"From the agitation in your manner, it seems to be a matter of some urgency."

"It is."

"A death penalty case, with the execution looming?"

Mrs. Humiston blanched and turned to me. "I've read your accounts of Mr. Holmes's cases, but I never really believed that his powers of deduction were that effective."

"Many other people have made similar comments over the decades, Mrs. Humiston," I replied. "I must say, my friend never tires of proving other people wrong."

"What is particularly vexing is the fact that many people seem positively desperate to receive confirmation that my powers of acumen are not as skillful as is commonly publicized. It seems that every week I come across someone who is positively crushed by the fact that I am able to figure out trifling details of their lives and habits." Holmes groaned softly and tented his fingertips. "I have no wish to discuss people's conceptions of me and my observational skills. A person has been condemned to death, correct?"

"Yes."

"And you are convinced that the person facing the gallows is innocent?"

"She's to face the electric chair, not the hangman's rope, but yes, I know in my heart that she had nothing to do with the murder."

"When is she scheduled to die?"

"In less than a week."

"That is a relief."

"I beg your pardon?"

For a brief moment, a flicker of embarrassment passed over Holmes's face. "I expressed myself badly. I feared that your client was to be executed tonight. I did not relish the prospect of a frantic rush to gather up enough evidence to earn a stay of execution at the very last moment."

Mrs. Humiston did not appear completely mollified. "I'm pleased that you won't have to rush your dinner and skip dessert."

Holmes showed no contrition in response to this remark. "Yes, it would be such a shame to travel across the Atlantic Ocean, visit a restaurant that came highly recommended by a longtime acquaintance, and be forced to rapidly consume my meal like a ravenous wolf. And as we're on the topic...." A waiter arrived at our table. "Will you be dining with us as our guest, Mrs. Humiston? You can provide us with the details of the case while we eat."

Mrs. Humiston looked a bit ruffled by the offer. "What? Oh, yes. I've dined here many times. The sole meunière is excellent. I shall have that."

Neither of us followed Mrs. Humiston on her recommendation. I ordered the Lobster Newberg, and Holmes selected the sirloin of beef with mashed potatoes and carrots.

As soon as the waiter had filled our water glasses, Mrs. Humiston took a deep sip and turned back to Holmes. "Have you heard about the Flora Blundell case?"

"I'm afraid I've been too busy resolving a rather delicate matter to follow the local papers."

"It hasn't been in the newspapers for some weeks. Not since poor Flora was convicted. As far as most of New York City is concerned, the whole affair is over. So there's no reason why you would have heard about it."

The waiter arrived with three bowls of consommé and set them before us. Mrs. Humiston scooped up a few drops and set them delicately in her mouth. "As you have probably heard, Mr. Holmes, I am the founder of the People's Law Firm. For over fifteen years, we have provided quality legal representation for the indigent and for immigrants who are struggling to survive in a strange country. Sometimes we provide services completely *pro bono*, and often we charge very modest fees that our clients can easily afford."

"Is that meant to be a subtle way of telling me that I should not expect much in the way of financial remuneration for my troubles?" Holmes asked dryly, but with a twinkle in his eye.

Mrs. Humiston looked taken aback. "If you can help me clear Flora's name, I will gladly pay whatever you ask out of my own pocket."

"I will not commit to anything at present. Please, continue."

"Flora worked as a barmaid at the Yellow Primrose. Despite the rather pretty name, it was a dark, seedy speakeasy in a residential area of the city. The liquor served there was cheap and watered-down, the lighting was almost non-existent, and of course, it's completely illegal under Prohibition. Flora's a nice girl, but it's hard to make a living, and serving at that horrid dive was the only way she could earn enough money to scrape by, you see."

"I would never condemn a young woman for taking a job as a barmaid. It's a perfectly acceptable way to keep body and soul together in London, and just because your government has seen fit to criminalize the sale of alcoholic beverages, I cannot say that I consider her work to be especially criminal."

"That is a welcome viewpoint to hear, Mr. Holmes. At her trial, the prosecutor made it sound like serving up a glass of bathtub gin was evidence of a complete lack of moral fiber, and he even made veiled insinuations that Flora was supplementing her income by performing certain … indecent actions with the male clientele. I can assure you that there was no truth to this whatsoever. It was simply a vile innuendo on the part of the prosecutor, utilized in the hopes of demonizing the defendant and causing the morally outraged men of the jury to vote 'guilty,' despite the fact that there was no solid evidence of her guilt."

"There were no witnesses, then? No direct physical proof that she had committed the crime?"

"None. It happened very late at night, half an hour after closing time at the Yellow Primrose. Flora, the bartender, and another barmaid were washing up the glasses and cleaning up the establishment for the night. The proprietor of the establishment, a Mr. Gideon Dorewell, collected the night's take and brought it downstairs into the basement to lock it away in his safe. This was standard operating procedure. Every night Mr. Dorewell would lock away the profits from the speakeasy, walk a block down the street to his apartment, and upon waking in the mid-afternoon, return to the speakeasy, take the money from the safe, and deposit it — or at least most of it — in the bank a quarter of a mile away. He was in the habit of carrying a revolver with him for protection."

Holmes finished the last of his soup, then stroked the tip of his chin. "But surely, Mr. Dorewell could not have deposited money into the bank every day."

"You are correct, Mr. Holmes. Banks are closed on Sundays, and by the time Mr. Dorewell usually awoke on Saturdays, his bank was shuttered, as it closed early that day. By Sunday night, the safe was filled with a weekend's worth of cash, as the proceeds from Friday, Saturday, and Sunday were in there. Every Monday, Mr. Dorewell would take all that money, stuff it all in a bag he had strapped to his chest, throw on an overcoat, and hurry as fast as he could to the bank, with one hand on the revolver in his pocket. Apparently, he had a much lighter overcoat for summer, though in any event wearing such a garment was bound to attract attention during the dog days."

"But he wasn't killed on the way to the bank."

"No. He was not. When Flora went downstairs to pick up a few more bottles of the establishment's best — to use the word loosely — product, she came downstairs and found Mr. Dorewell lying dead on the floor. He'd been hit over the head with a bottle, and his body was in front of the open safe. The safe was not empty — there was still a large quantity of money in it, although when the bartender examined it, he thought that there was somewhat less than there ought to have been, though he couldn't be sure, as they don't keep very careful records in that business."

The waiter brought a platter of paté, olives, and triangles of toast. Holmes and I both helped ourselves, but Mrs. Humiston left it untouched. After taking what he wanted, Holmes remarked, "It seems to me reasonable to suppose that when the police investigated, they found no one else in the basement, and — as Mr. Dorewell went down there alone, and Flora was the only one to follow him there — they assumed that she murdered him."

"Exactly! Isn't it ridiculous? They believe that she went down there, hit him over the head, and then just ran upstairs screaming, claiming that she found him there, dead."

"It's not a totally irrational supposition. So far as the police could tell, it was just her there. No one else had the opportunity."

"But what could be the motive?" I asked.

Mrs. Humiston groaned. "The police believe that Flora was trying to steal money from the safe. Mr. Dorewell caught her, perhaps he fired her, and in a blind rage she supposedly struck him with the bottle. Then she ran upstairs in a state of shock, not realizing that no one else could be blamed for the crime."

90

"On the face of it, it sounds reasonable. But did they find any fingerprints on the bottle? Any blood on Flora's clothing? Did she waver in protesting her innocence for even a second?"

"No! Not for one moment!" Mrs. Humiston groaned and picked up an olive. "Mr. Holmes, I tell you that I believe in Flora one hundred per cent. I have dedicated my life to protecting people who cannot help themselves, even when the authorities care little for them. To most of society, women like Flora do not matter. She is not very intelligent, she is nowhere near beautiful, and if we are to be honest, left to her own devices her life would not be an especially distinctive one, though one can hope that she will find happiness in it. Her life will almost certainly be one of poverty and hard work. She's a kind person, and it's possible she could meet a decent man. Perhaps she could find love and have children. Surely that's a pleasant enough future."

"I am told that many people deem a life like the one you describe as a totally acceptable fate."

"But she will have no happy ending in the death house, Mr. Holmes. I just found out about her case a couple of weeks ago, and I've thought of nothing but rescuing her ever since."

"You didn't handle her defense at the trial, then?" I asked.

"No. Her lawyer did his best, I suppose. He tried to argue that Dorewell had made improper advances toward her, and that she'd hit him over the head in order to defend her honor."

I shrugged. "A plea of self-defense sounds like a sensible plan."

"Unfortunately, Flora would have none of it. She insisted on pleading 'not guilty' without any qualifier, and when her lawyer tried to suggest the situation I just described to the jury, she stood up and yelled, 'No, no, no, no! That didn't happen! I never touched him!' She demanded to be put on the stand to tell her story, but the poor girl is very highly strung. When the prosecutor cross-examined her she fell to pieces and started crying. I suppose the jury took that as an admission of guilt."

Our main courses arrived, and as Holmes picked up his fork and knife, he said, "It would help me if I could see the scene of the crime."

"I'm afraid you can't visit the actual Yellow Primrose. It burned to the ground not long after the murder."

"I wondered why you used the past tense when describing it," Holmes commented.

"I can, however, show you these photographs," Mrs. Humiston added. She drew a large envelope from her purse. "These should give you a good idea of what the basement looked like."

Holmes swallowed a bite of beef. "Do you have any pictures of the deceased?"

"Well, yes, but you're eating."

Cutting himself another piece of meat, Holmes replied, "And why should that matter in the slightest?"

Mrs. Humiston opened her mouth to speak, apparently thought better of it, and then handed the envelope to Holmes. After a few moments of rustling around in her purse, she found a second, smaller envelope and passed it to Holmes as well. "I also have a copy of the autopsy report in here."

"I shall need a few minutes to focus, please," Holmes said. He took out the photographs and sorted through them one at a time, continuing to eat his food as he examined the evidence. Mrs. Humiston and I silently ate our dinners as well. By the time Holmes had finished scrutinizing all of the pictures, all of our plates were nearly clean.

"How tall is Flora?" Holmes finally asked.

"A shade over five feet tall, but strongly built."

"Hmm. According to the autopsy report, Mr. Dorewell was five foot nine. His head was totally bald, which makes it easier to see the wounds. The photographs of the body indicate that the deceased was struck directly over the head. The killer must have been significantly taller than Dorewell. At least six foot two, I should say, if not more."

"Perhaps he was kneeling on the ground," I ventured.

"I considered that possibility, but the photographs indicate that the floor of the basement was covered with dust and mud. Dorewell fell on his side when he was killed. I see no stains on the knees of his trousers. Was this point brought up at the trial?"

"It was not," Mrs. Humiston looked hopeful. "This is a start. Perhaps it's enough to ask the Governor for clemency."

"Let's wait for a little while. There is still the question of how the actual killer got in and out of the basement. You never had a chance to examine the Yellow Primrose yourself before it burned?"

"No. I should mention that Mr. Kron has been performing his own investigation into the fire."

"It's arson, then?"

"It's a strong possibility. Two men were seen carrying large metal canisters away from the Yellow Primrose right after the conflagration started. Mr. Kron and I think that if we find the arsonists, it may help lead us to the real killer."

"Take a look at these photographs, Watson." Holmes passed the pictures to me. "Do you see anything of note?"

I did not. There were several shelves throughout the room filled with bottles of various sizes and labels. There were six large barrels on their sides, resting on stands against one wall, and some lanterns were hanging from hooks on the ceiling.

"Unfortunately, the police inadvertently destroyed crucial evidence when they searched the crime scene. They walked around the basement, and in the dim light, they did not see the footprints they were erasing."

"Footprints?"

"In the dust and mud, in front of the barrels, you can just barely see a footprint pointing directly at that barrel on the end."

I looked closely at the barrel. "Nothing sinister about that. Someone walked up to the barrel to pour a pitcher of beer. I didn't know that American speakeasies were smuggling in beer from France. *Bière Échappatoire.*"

"More likely, they've been taking alcohol across the Canadian border. They voted against prohibition there in 1919. Some people have been going there for liquor," Mrs. Humiston explained.

"I have learned French from spending time with my relatives, the Vernets. 'Échappatoire' translates to 'exit' or 'way out.' " Holmes smiled. "I know that many speakeasies make a point of concealing passageways in their establishments in case of a raid. I believe that the barrel is a carefully designed door that leads into a tunnel. I have no idea who committed the murder, nor do I know for certain what the motive was, but that's how the true killer got in and out of the basement."

Before either of us could respond, the waiter approached the table. "Mr. Holmes, will you, your wife, or Dr. Watson care for any dessert?"

"She is *not* my wife!" Holmes replied with such intense firmness that the formerly implacable waiter sidled away so quickly that I was compelled to rise from my chair and follow him in order to request the menu for puddings.

"None for me," Mrs. Humiston told us as she gathered up all the photographs into her purse. "I have to talk to Mr. Kron and get him to look into this."

"They may have burned the Yellow Primrose," Holmes commented, "but I dare say that the end of the tunnel can still be found in the basement of the building next door. "That hasn't been burned, has it?"

"No. It's a private home."

"Then I would not be surprised if a member of that household was responsible for the killing."

Mrs. Humiston agreed, thanked us, and hurried away after a very brief set of goodbyes. As I enjoyed my charlotte russe, I asked Holmes, "Do you think that will be enough to save that poor Flora woman?"

"I hope so. Of course, it never hurts to exercise a little bit of influence wherever possible. My recent investigation has brought me into contact with gentlemen in high places. A word or two to them may lead to helpful results."

*   *   *

The next afternoon, Holmes and I were packing our suitcases, preparing for our voyage back to England. A bellhop knocked at the door, delivering a envelope addressed to Holmes. Tearing it open, Holmes read aloud:

My dear Mr. Holmes:

I cannot possibly express all the gratitude that I feel toward you, but I hope that this letter will serve as a start. You were quite right about the secret tunnel. Mr. Kron was able to enter the house next door to the former Yellow Primrose disguised as a plumber (I won't tell you about the little subterfuge we had to use in order to convince the housekeeper to let him inside). While there, he uncovered the tunnel in the basement. A little more digging revealed that the owner of the house, a greengrocer named Mr. Munderman, enjoys a lifestyle far more luxurious than that of the average shopkeeper. Mr. Kron's informants explained that Mr. Munderman has long been suspected of being a pivotal player in the illegal liquor importing business from Canada to New York City. When Mr. Kron confronted the housekeeper with his discovery, she quickly broke down. Apparently, she'd witnessed Mr. Dorewell visiting the house on numerous occasions, and the night before the murder, Dorewell had an argument with Mr. Munderman and his son. She couldn't hear much distinctly, but she did catch the phrase "skimming off the top." I believe that Dorewell was taking more than his share of the proceeds, and since Mr. Munderman is five foot eight while his son is six foot three, I'm sure that it was the son who committed the actual crime, though it was the father who ordered the arson to prevent anyone from discovering the passageway. I dare say that this was not a premeditated murder. Mr. Munderman's son probably slipped through the secret passageway to confront Dorewell about stealing money, and the two men fought, and Mr. Munderman's son killed him in a fit of rage. Mr. Munderman seems like a sensible businessman, who never would have had his business partner killed next door to his own home. Mr. Kron's investigation indicated that certain precautions had been taken to assure that the fire did not spread to the Munderman residence. The authorities are in the process of gathering evidence, but in the meantime, I have been assured by the governor that dear Flora is in no danger of being executed. Once again, thank you so much, Mr. Holmes.

Sincerely,

Grace Quackenbos Humiston

P.S. Again, I must apologize for people's false belief that we are married. I feel thankful that my husband Howard is more amused by this than annoyed.

"It seems as though this matter has come to a satisfactory conclusion," I informed Holmes. Before he could reply, there was another knock at the door, revealing a different bellhop bringing me the afternoon paper. "Oh, dear," I said as I rifled through the pages.

"What's the matter, Watson?"

"Look at this." I handed him the newspaper, folded back to the society pages. There was an image of Holmes and Mrs. Humiston there, though I had been cropped out of the photograph. The headline read, "Mr. and Mrs. Sherlock Holmes Enjoy Dinner Together."

Holmes threw down the paper with a disgusted groan and once again made it clear to me that my account of this case would be consigned to a battered tin dispatch-box for a very long time. "I trust that you will not release the details of this case to your readers, Watson. I do not wish for false rumors of my marriage to spread across the Atlantic."

The Search for Mycroft's Successor

As much as it pains me to admit it, none of us are immortal. Sooner or later we all must leave this world and face whatever comes next. In the months following the Armistice at the end of the Great War, I found that I was not the only one reflecting on the fact that all of our times must come to an end. While every life has value, some admittedly have a deeper impact than others on the fates of nations. This was the case with Mycroft, Holmes' elder brother.

When a monarch dies, the heir to the throne is always in waiting. As much as Britons may revere their best kings and queens, deep in all of our minds is the unspoken realization that all crowned heads are replaceable, and the line of succession is well-known. But there are other individuals who are genuinely and unquestionably indispensable. One such man is Holmes' brother Mycroft.

Mycroft invited us to his rooms a few months after the signing of the Treaty of Versailles. It was a time when most were relieved, even jubilant, in the knowledge that the long years of war were over, and peace was restored. From the expression on Mycroft's face, he was nowhere near relaxed. His eyes had the fog of a man who had not slept as much as he ought to have, and his clothes appeared rather tight, as if the already corpulent man had turned to his favorite foods in order to assuage the stress that was evident in his demeanor.

Holmes sized up his brother's mental state with a swift up and down glance. "I can see that you have been worrying lately, my dear brother."

"Can you blame me, brother Sherlock?"

"I most certainly cannot. The last four years have been a terrible strain for most people. It must have been exponentially horrible for the man who at times, to all intents and purposes, *is* the British Government."

"The world could have been spared a great many needless deaths and sleepless nights if the Prime Minister had not sidelined me at the worst possible time in 1914," Mycroft groaned. "Those fools informed me that they had no further need of my services, gave me a miniscule pension and a gold watch that loses two minutes every hour, and then, not two weeks after the start of hostilities, called me back to work without so much as a "please." I have spent the last four years trying to clean up their messes and prevent the nation from crumbling, and now that the wretched war has finally ended, those silly diplomats have put together a so-called "peace" treaty that will lead to yet another massive war within a generation. Possibly I may be able to assuage the situation, or maybe delay the horrors for several more years, but I doubt it very much." Mycroft sagged back in his chair, and he looked far older, more exhausted, and weaker than I had ever seen him.

"Cheer up," I informed him. "I'm sure that all will turn out for the best."

I had never seen so much pure contempt in Mycroft's face. "No, Watson, it will *not* be all right! I am not a particularly vain man, but I know for a fact that without me, England will not be able to withstand another terrible war. I am not flattering myself when I assert that my presence is necessary to the nation's survival. And I will not live forever. I have never fussed much over my health, and it is too late to start now. I may have another year or two in me, perhaps another couple of decades if I am extraordinarily lucky, but eventually, I will meet my Maker and there will be no one to take my place. We cannot trust our statesmen to handle the increasingly volatile situation. I need a replacement for myself. I cannot rest until I know that when I finally pass on, the nation will be in sound hands. I am too busy with my work to launch a search of my own. That is why I have summoned you today. Find my successor. Search England for the best and the brightest, and when you believe that you have found as man– a *young* man, mind you, one who will be able to handle this job for decades to come– and convince him to come work for me. We need someone with a mind sufficiently clever and dexterous to handle all of the complexities connected to managing the intricacies of the British government. This is a full-time job, so we need someone willing to devote his entire life to this project, preferably one who is content to forgo the distractions of a wife and children as well so he can focus on his work."

Mycroft shifted his weight in his chair, and took a long sip from a glass of water on the table next to him. "I have never regretted not marrying, at least, not until now. Perhaps I might have had a son who could have taken over this position. Then again, I might have been too overwhelmed by the duties of fatherhood to have saved England from hundreds of near disasters. In any case, dear brother, you know as well as I do that intelligence of the kind that the two of us possess does not necessarily pass from father to son. We have many clever fellows in our family, and one or two might make fine detectives like yourself, but none of them have the brain stamina and calculating abilities to take over my role in the government. In any event, it's likely that I might have sired an utter dunderhead, fit for nothing more cranially strenuous that the easy life of a country squire. And that would have done us no good whatsoever in this situation."

"Have you come across anybody in your work who might be able to take on the duties of your protégé, Mycroft?" Holmes asked.

"None. The British Civil Service is filled with a handful of smart men and a great many workaday pudding-heads. Many are called out of a sincere desire to serve their country, but men of the kind of inspired genius that we need are nonexistent." Mycroft drank more water. "I trust that you will not think me arrogant by using that word to describe the brainpower that is essential for this position, but it is a simple fact that one needs a certain kind of mind to handle the facts, figures, and intricacies of my job. When I created this position for myself, I observed a need and chose to fill it myself. At the time, I did not realize how essential I would become to the wellbeing of England, not did I ever suspect the seeming impossibility of teaching someone else how to perform this job. But it *must* be done, and you, brother, are the only one who has the wherewithal to find a worthy man."

"Or woman," I suggested.

"Don't be ridiculous," Mycroft snapped at me.

"Do you have any suggestions on how to proceed, Mycroft?" Holmes asked.

"Nothing that will significantly improve success. I know of only three young men who *might* have the brains to take on the position, and one is from southern China, another lives in northern India, and the third calls the American Midwest home. But they are all loyal to their current nations, and two of them already have large families. None of them will be persuaded to come to England and serve our interests. That means that you can limit your search to our country. I have started a study of the students and recent graduates of our nation's universities and best schools, and though we have lots of able men…"

"None of them are what we are looking for," Holmes finished.

"Precisely. And you, dear brother, would not find my intellectually stimulating yet physically sedentary job to your tastes. Is there no one of your acquaintance that springs to mind?"

"No specific living person. There was one man who might have managed this epic task, but he chose to devote his incredible abilities to more destructive habits. However…"

"Of course!" A glint flashed in Mycroft's eyes. "I wondered if you would consider that possibility, Sherlock. It is possible that a member of his extended family might be up to the task, if genetics are any guide. Which, as I mentioned earlier, is not always the case."

"But we must be careful. While some of them may have the ability, I doubt that most of them have the character necessary for the job. Indeed, that is the curse of that family. The decent, moral members of that family uniformly have pedestrian, mediocre minds. In contrast, the most brilliant individuals with the moniker in question are dangerous. Upon reflection, I can think of one man from that family, who at thirty-nine is probably not too old for our purposes, who could very likely learn how to take over your job… but he would use it to take over the nation as well. Within ten years, Parliament would be his puppets, and he would be the dictator of England, and possibly of most of Western Europe as well."

"You have maintained your files on that family?"

"Of course. I am forever on the lookout for the possibility that one will follow in their patriarch's infamous footsteps."

"Excuse me, but which family are you talking about?" I asked with a touch of irritation.

Holmes glanced at me with mild surprise. "The Moriarty family, Watson. Who else would we be discussing?"

Holmes went into another room and spent ten minutes making telephone calls. Soon afterwards, the two of us were in a car heading to the West End. "Holmes, are you seriously considering turning over England's security and stability to a Moriarty?"

"I can assure, Watson, that I am not exploring this possibility lightly. No one is more aware than I am of how dangerous a Moriarty can be. I am also aware that while intelligence may be passed on from one generation to the next, there is no scientific proof that criminality is inherited as well. In any case, most of the Moriarty family is composed of harmless blockheads. Colonel James Moriarty was a man of no great ability, but he rose in the ranks thanks to the well-hidden intervention of his brother, the Professor. The Colonel's main claim to fame is an insistence that his brother was completely innocent, and that I am a malicious fool who slandered an innocent man. Their other brother, the stationmaster James–"

"I can't understand why the Moriarty family named all three brothers James."

"It is a family tradition. Most male members of the family go by their middle names. In any case, Stationmaster James is as decent enough man, who has no particular aptitude for anything in particular save for crossword puzzles. Meanwhile, the children of Colonel and Stationmaster have reached adulthood, and their mental abilities are a mixed bag. Both brothers have three children. The Colonel has two daughters, one of whom is an amiable featherbrain, and the other is woman of rare intelligence who is unhappily married to a philanderer. I might consider this woman for the position, were it not for the fact that she has devised no less than four brilliant schemes to murder her husband and put the blame on his latest mistress, and it is only thorough my own fortunate intervention that her plans have never succeeded. The couple has separated many times, yet for reasons I cannot understand, a reconciliation inevitably follows a couple of weeks later."

"And the Colonel's third child is a son?"

"Yes. James Albert Moriarty is an actor, and he is currently taking on a part that is made for him– the role of his uncle, Professor Moriarty in one of those endless revivals of that play by William Gillette very loosely based on my career."

"An actor? Do you really think that he has the ability to replace Mycroft?"

"I grant you that his talents lie in the creative arts, but he is surprisingly talented. His Iago was a minor sensation, and he has risen to fame as a skilled portrayer of villains. I have attended a couple of his performances before the war, and he has a certain amount of charisma, but more important, he has imagination. I believe that he is consistently able to bring a fresh and innovative approach to a well-known character, which shows a certain level of innovation and an ability to take the familiar and make it fresh."

"Do you really think that ability could be applied to handling the affairs of government?"

"It has been my experience, Watson, that creativity is a great asset when it is combined with logic and extensive knowledge. Albert– I shall refer to him by his middle name for the sake of clarity– has never been to university, and he is primarily an autodidact. I know that he studied the history of ancient Rome extensively for his preparation of the role of Brutus in *Julius Caesar*. He served in the military before being wounded and sent home after four months, and he has no known attachments, either romantic or those of ordinary friendship. His fellow actors consider him talented but distant. He is respected as a thespian but not particularly well-liked as a person."

"But can an actor perform Mycroft's duties?"

"From what I've heard, he has taken an active role in the management duties of one performing company, where he managed to clean up their financial situation and eliminated their debt. A stunning achievement, especially for those working in the dramatic arts. Again, I need to view this with some skepticism. There may be something less than honest behind the company's sudden solvency. We shall see."

Moments later, we arrived at a small, shabby-looking theater and walked inside. When we asked to see Albert Moriarty (it should be noted that he performed under a stage name, but for reasons of clarity I have chosen to refer to him by his real moniker), we were told he had not yet arrived, but would in half an hour. Holmes asked to wait in the manager's office, and after slipping the stage manager two one-pound notes, we were allowed inside.

"What are you looking for?" I asked as Holmes started rifling through the papers on a desk.

As he withdrew a ledger from under a stack of assorted playbills and posters, Holmes explained, "Financial records. If this is what I hope to find…" His voice trailed off as he flipped through the pages, running his finger along columns. I could see the calculations flashing in his eyes as he totaled the numbers in his mind.

I said nothing for nearly thirty minutes, until a knock on the door snapped Holmes out of his reflections, and he shoved the ledger back under a pile of paper just as the door opened. The stage manager informed us that the man we were looking for had arrived, and we were led to a dimly lit dressing room.

Albert Moriarty was sprawled out in a chair, with a silver-headed cane across his knees. "Ah! Sherlock Holmes! Have you come to play yourself on the stage? That certainly would be a boon to ticket sales. I wish I'd thought of it earlier."

"That is not why I am here," Holmes said as he lowered himself onto a rickety-looking bench. I did not think that it would support my weight as well, so I leaned against the corner walls.

"A pity. I should have liked to have been paired against you on the stage. And you as well, Dr. Watson," he told me with an expression that I thought was a combination of a leer and a sneer. "Wouldn't it be wonderful to have the three of us on stage together? You as yourselves, and me as my illustrious relative?"

"Illustrious?" I snorted.

Albert shrugged. "I chose my words without much thought. He was a magnificent man, even if he was a criminal. Most of our politicians are like that. Power-hungry, unscrupulous, and caring nothing for other people. Yet because they have managed to persuade people to cast ballots for them, they are respected, while my relative is now one of history's greatest villains. He could have been Prime Minister if he'd set his mind that way. But he wouldn't have been happy pandering to constituents or his party. He'd have much preferred to have been king, but monarchs don't have any real power these days anyway. So maybe it was best that he made his mark on the world in the way he did."

"As a criminal and murderer?" I asked before I could regain control of the tone of my voice.

Luckily, Albert didn't seem offended. "Well, if you're going to be judgmental about it..." He leaned back in his chair and kicked up his legs, resting his feet on the ends of the table.

Holmes stood up with a little groan. "Thank you for seeing us. We'll be leaving now."

"Will you be coming to see the show tonight?"

"No."

"Aren't you going to tell me to break a leg?"

"I think you've had quite enough damage to your legs, haven't you? Good day." Holmes strode out of the dressing-room with impressive speed, and I followed him back to the car.

Holmes was clearly in a sour humor, and I said nothing for several minutes, until the awkwardness overwhelmed my desire to allow him the quiet time he so deeply appreciates. "Well? What was wrong with him?"

"Where to start?"

"How about the ledger? There was clearly something wrong with that."

"Indeed. The totals make it look like the dramatic company's in sound financial health, which is suspicious in itself. In any case, I performed some simple arithmetic, and it seems as if their debts have been paid off with nonexistent funds."

"I don't understand. How is that possible?"

"Simply put, Alfred has created a financial house of cards. It allows for seeming prosperity for a limited period of time, but everything will fall apart eventually, and at that point, the company will be totally bankrupt, and even though Alfred is responsible for the financial malfeasance, he won't be on the hook for the debts himself."

"Are you sure he's behind the… creative accounting?"

"The handwriting on the ledger matches the scribbles on a script in his dressing-room."

"What was that comment you made about his leg?"

"You remember I mentioned he was injured and invalided out of the war?"

"Yes."

"And he carries the cane as an affectation. He doesn't really need it. But when he raised his leg, I saw his trouser leg slide back enough to see the wound caused by the bullet that sent him home from the front."

"I didn't get a close enough look at it to examine it properly."

"That is understandable. Had you been able to apply your trained medical eyes to it, you would have discovered that from the angle of the scarring, his wound was almost certainly self-inflicted. He shot himself with a handgun, just badly enough to be released from his duties."

"What a coward."

"Well, enough young men saw such terrible horrors on the front lines that I cannot judge them too harshly for wanting to escape with their lives. Still, combined with his accounting, it shows a distinct lack of character. Possibly with sufficient guidance and influence he could be molded into what we are looking for, but he's over thirty now and far too old for his character to be reshaped. Had he received proper training at a younger age, he could have replaced Mycroft eventually. As it is now, his moral compass is too shaky for us to trust him with anything. I suppose I should tell the owners of the theater to hire a proper accountant to examine the books to find out just how deep a hole they're currently in, and we'll see what happens. I doubt that Alfred will learn a lesson, though. I saw no signs of conscience or contrition in his face. He is clearly off the list."

"So where are we off to now, Holmes?"

"The Old Bailey, Watson, to speak to James Walter Moriarty. He is the elder son of Stationmaster James. Walter is a barrister of moderate reputation who specializes in criminal cases."

"Are any of his clients connected to his uncle?"

"A few low-level miscreants. Petty thieves and brutal lads who fell into the Professor's webs as youths and grew up to be inept professional criminals who spend their wasted lives drifting in and out of prison. No one of particular interest to me. Walter does, however, defend the occasional client of means, and is able to make a simple living off of these fees."

"Is a mediocre barrister our best hope of finding a successor for Mycroft?"

"I doubt it. Yet Walter intrigues me. According to my records, Walter was a brilliant student and on track to become one of the most celebrated attorneys of his generation. And now he languishes in relative obscurity. I wonder why this is the case."

"Perhaps his excellent grades were the result of cheating, and he was unable to find a similar path to success in the workforce."

"That is suspicious-minded of you, Watson, but what you say is not impossible. The only way to find out for certain what is behind his undistinguished to career is to meet with him."

Soon afterwards, we arrived at the Old Bailey, and were informed that Walter was still in court, but he would be finished for the day soon. Not wishing to wait any longer than necessary, Holmes and I quietly entered the courtroom where the case Walter was defending was being heard, and found seats in the gallery.

We arrived in the middle of Walter's summation to the jury. "–it is clear that the prosecution has failed to prove beyond a reasonable doubt that my client was responsible for the thefts. Their sole witness is an elderly man with a degenerative eye condition. There is no proof that the pound notes in his pockets were not his own, won earlier that evening in a card game. Furthermore–"

At this point, Holmes nudged me, and we both exited the courtroom. "I've seen enough," Holmes told me as soon as the door had closed behind us.

"We were there less than thirty seconds."

"More than enough time for me to determine the reason for Walter's middling career. I could see it in his eyes. He has contracted pupils and a skin pallor... he's a drug addict, Watson."

I nodded. "I observed what you did. He's clearly not a well man. I would say that he has been abusing drugs for years."

"While I am in no position to criticize a man who is addicted to drugs, I can state definitively that such a man should not be considered for a position as important as Mycroft's."

I chose my next words very carefully. "Holmes, are you... absolutely certain that Mycroft's role is absolutely necessary? After all, England survived for centuries without him. Other countries appear to be functioning fine without men like Mycroft behind the scenes." A thought struck me. "At least... I *think* that other countries don't have men like Mycroft performing vital roles out of the sight of the average citizen. I could be wrong."

"I'm afraid you are, Watson. Most of the world's great powers have their own versions of Mycroft, though to the best of my knowledge, most of them are not nearly as skilled as my brother. And it is not an exaggeration to say that Mycroft's temporary sidelining was directly responsible for the Great War. The Boer War only occurred because Mycroft was laid up for three weeks with influenza. If Mycroft dies, and we have no one to replace him, it will lead to disaster on a global scale."

"After all we've endured with the Great War, no one will want another conflict on that magnitude," I assured Holmes.

"That may be at the heart of the problem, Watson. If one side is determined to avoid another war, a belligerent nation may be able to extract concessions up to the point where either the other country will fall, or will be forced to fight. Either possibility is unacceptable."

"Then do all of our hopes rely on Stationmaster James' younger son?"

"Unless you can think of an alternative, you are correct. He is known as J.J."

"J.J." I mulled over this for a moment. "No, his parents couldn't possibly have named him–"

"They did. James James."

"Why?"

"The Moriarty family is an odd one, full of eccentricities and inside jokes, as well as copious amounts of brilliance and twisted psyches. It's quite possible that J.J.'s father considered this a great joke. It's also within the bounds of probability that it was some sort of sadistic plan to make sure the boy would be mocked by his schoolfellows. I cannot tell at present. I can say that J.J. has taken it upon himself to follow in the footsteps of his uncle, the Colonel, and become the protector of his family name."

"How so?"

"You are not the only one to take an interest in writing about my cases, Watson. Shortly before the war, J.J. wrote a lengthy book in defense of his uncle, arguing that dear old Uncle James was nothing more than a misunderstood, slandered academic who was framed by a cocaine-addled, overrated, incompetent consulting detective."

"But surely he must have realized that you weren't trying to slander the Professor."

"Oh, J.J.'s book posited that I was sincere enough in my convictions. His thesis is that Colonel Sebastian Moran was the real mastermind of the criminal gang, and the Professor was nothing more than a sacrificial lamb- an innocent man plucked from obscurity to serve as a dupe. J.J. reached out to several publishers, but none would touch it. One of them informed me of the manuscript, and after reading it, I realized that J.J. had a brilliant and creative mind, even if his conclusions were utter tommyrot. I confronted him shortly before the war began and tried to persuade him that he was mistaken, but he did not take kindly to my arguments, and became quite enraged by what I had to say. He has a terrible temper, which is why I put him at the bottom of the list. Still, it's possible that the years have mellowed him."

"Where is he now?"

"He was a medic during the war. According to my informant that I telephoned earlier, he is currently at the Dunstable Hospital. Perhaps he has become a doctor, or at least an orderly. We shall see."

Half an hour later we arrived at the Dunstable Hospital, a grim and unsettling place on the outskirts of London, surrounded by massive walls. After some cajoling, Holmes was allowed to speak to the head nurse.

"Why do you want to see Mr. Moriarty?" she asked.

"I wish to interview him about a job," Holmes replied.

"He will not be able to accept any position you offer."

"Is he under contract at this hospital?"

"You misunderstand me. He is a patient here."

A sudden flash of realization passed over my face. "This hospital… it is an asylum."

"Yes. Mr. Moriarty had a breakdown three years into the war. The doctors have done their best, but they believe that he is incurable…"

This news left Holmes looking desolate. He said nothing as we rode back to our hotel, and he refused to join me for dinner. He locked himself in his room, and I heard no more from him until after breakfast the following morning, when he emerged looking disheveled and unslept, but triumphant.

"I may have a solution to our problem, Watson," he said as he buttered a piece of cold toast that had been brought to his room hours earlier. "It is unwieldy, but it could serve our purposes adequately."

"What is it?"

"I need a few more minutes to refine my ideas. In half an hour we have a meeting with Mycroft and a representative from the government, a Mr. Chumbley. Apparently he is well-connected and has the ear of the Prime Minister. You will learn all when we meet with them."

Thirty minutes later, we were gathered in Mycroft's rooms, as the young, lean, dour-looking Mr. Chumbley glared at us. "Why did you wish to speak to me?"

"You are aware of how indispensable my brother is to the workings of the British government. In matters of foreign policy, spycraft, economics, domestic affairs, and other issues, he is absolutely vital. When he dies, which will hopefully not be for many more years, England will be crippled. If a replacement for my brother exists, I do not know of him. Then I realized, if no one man can replace Mycroft, perhaps several can. Consider this. A specialist or team of experts, maybe two or three, each handling one aspect of what Mycroft does. I have broken Mycroft's duties down into seven fields. I have adjusted the wording for reasons that will become evident once you read the first letter of each topic." Holmes withdrew a piece of paper from his pocket and set it on the table in front of Mr. Chumbley. It read:

MILITARY STRATEGY

YEOMANRY

COMMERCE AND CURRENCY

ROYAL ISSUES

OMBUDSMAN

FOREIGN AFFAIRS

TRADECRAFT

"Think of it," Holmes explained. "The brightest minds in their fields, all contributing to do the work that Mycroft does now. A secret team of the cleverest men in the country, all working in their respective topics for the good of the nation. It would…" Holmes' voice trailed off as he caught Mycroft's eye.

"Not a bad idea, brother," Mycroft sighed. "But I came up with something very similar months ago. Only without the silly acrostic."

"And I rejected it then and will again," Mr. Chumbley replied. "We already have quite enough supposed geniuses on the government payroll. There is no need to hire more."

"But who will replace–"

"People higher up than me put a great deal of faith in your brother. I do not share this high opinion. When he retires or dies, or once his patrons in the upper echelons of the British government are no longer there to protect him, the work he does will cease."

"But Mycroft is—"

"He's a relic! A superannuated fat fossil who has no place in the modern world. He should have died of a heart attack years ago. We don't need him!"

"Mr. Chumbley and I have a history," Mycroft growled. "I proved a few years ago that his wife was leaking secrets to a paramour in the German government."

"It's a lie!"

"It's the truth. Your wife is a traitor and an adulteress and you are a fool for shielding her. But as you see, dear brother, Mr. Chumbley resents me, and due to his parentage, he is extremely well-connected and has been placed in a position of power he has not earned and does not deserve."

Chumbley rose. "Insult me all you want. My friends in the government agree with me. You are no longer necessary. The world is too complex for the British government to rely upon the caprices of an old-fashioned man like yourself. Our current crop of politicians, diplomats, and civil service employees can handle the workings of the country perfectly well without one enormous crank telling us what we can and cannot do. We forced you into retirement once, Mycroft. I will do what I can to make sure you are put out to pasture again and stay there. Good day to you all." With that, Chumbley flounced out and left the room.

After a few moments I spoke. "Well. What do we do now?"

"Sit back and watch the world burn," Mycroft seethed. "I've made too many enemies, especially amongst the younger generation. They don't like me and they don't want me in a position of power."

"But does that mean that they'd be willing to harm the nation to spite you?"

"They genuinely believe that I'm no longer necessary," Mycroft sighed. "In any event, they're jealous of the power I hold and they want it for themselves."

"What will this mean for the future of the nation?" I wondered.

Holmes pressed his hand against his forehead. "I'm very much afraid that it means that the future of Europe is not as bright as we may have hoped. Without someone performing Mycroft's duties at Mycroft's level of competence, I believe that another Great War is inevitable…"

I felt utterly despondent. "So there's nothing we can do?"

Mycroft shrugged. "Sherlock and I will continue to look for a solution, but if the fools in the government continue to resist, they may cause the annihilation of another generation."

Holmes nodded. "For now, unfortunately, you must view this case as one of my failures."

As I write these words, I hope that someday I will be able to pen a conclusion to this case that proves that Holmes' statement was wrong. I have never before wished so desperately that one of our investigations will have a sequel.

The Outline of Mystery

(AUTHOR'S NOTE: The claims of the lawsuit at the center of this story really were alleged. The other crime that takes place in this story is completely fictional, and though most of the characters in this story are based on real-life people, the purely made-up creations will be identified at the end of the tale.)

Sherlock Holmes was happily analyzing a sample of honey. His bees had produced an abundant amount that year, but recently he had noticed that a heretofore absent shade of red had entered the honey after straining, and he was determined to seek out the cause. Could it be due to some new species of flower, not native to the Sussex Downs, that one of his neighbors had planted? Or could there be some sort of contamination affecting the honey? There was no discernable change to the taste or consistency, and Holmes found himself enjoying his chemical analysis. It was therefore quite vexing to him when his research was interrupted with a loud series of knocks at his door.

Not being in the mood to interact with anybody, Holmes decided that the best course of action was to ignore the knocking, but the pounding continued, and his best attempts to keep his attention focused on the honey were permanently thwarted by the sound of a woman's voice calling out, "Mr. Holmes! Mr. Holmes! Please! I know you're in there! I must speak to you!"

Holmes considered his options, and decided that a direct approach was best. He turned off the flame, jotted down a quick note, and crossed over to the door, opening it as the knocking was growing faster. The woman on the other side of the door was in the process of rapping her fist against the door again, and had Holmes not taken a quick step backwards he might have been struck in the chest.

"Mr. Holmes?" The woman was in her mid-sixties, with neatly arranged grey hair and wearing inexpensive but well cared-for garments. "My name is Florence Deeks. I must speak to you immediately!"

"Miss Deeks, I can tell that you are in a state of some agitation, but I must inform you that I am long retired from the business of private detection. I enjoy a quiet life and regrettably, at my age– I am nearly eighty– I cannot investigate as I did in my younger days."

"Please, Mr. Holmes! I have nowhere else to turn to. The courts have failed me. The government thinks I'm a hysterical old fool, the newspapers refuse to hear what I have to say, and now, even members of my own family have turned against me. I have nowhere else to go, and now I'm afraid that I will be arrested for murder! They've taken everything from me– my book, my reputation, and nearly all of my money. If you don't help me, I'll be thrown into jail and possibly hanged. I have nowhere else to turn. I have lost every scrap of faith I once had in our legal system, Mr. Holmes. If you shut the door on me, I shall sit down on your doorstep and I will not leave until the police come to take me away for a crime I did not commit. You are my only chance at justice. Please, sir, you must listen to me!"

Irritation was Holmes' primary emotion at that moment, but despite himself he also felt a genuine sense of sympathy towards Miss Deeks. Whether he wanted to or not, it was likely that he would be drawn into whatever situation she was entangled in, and he decided that despite his personal inclinations, he might as well grant her the opportunity to speak her piece.

"Miss Deeks, I shall make you a deal. I will give you five minutes of my valuable time for you to explain yourself. When that time has passed– and I will cut you off mid-sentence if I have to– I will tell you whether or not I am interested in hearing more. If I do not wish to hear any more of your story, I will tell you as much and you will be on your way. Do I have your word that you will follow the terms of this agreement?"

"Yes, Mr. Holmes, of course."

Holmes sighed and stepped away from the door, gesturing towards a pair of armchairs as he did so. Miss Deeks hung her coat upon a free hook, and as she was sitting down, Holmes commented, "I suppose at this point you are wondering if you would have been better off staying in Ontario."

"How did you know I was Canadian, Mr. Holmes?"

"Your accent, of course. I can also tell that you have been living in England for quite some time, judging from the type and amount of coal dust that has worked its way into your coat. But you don't live alone– you share lodgings with another woman– your sister, perhaps?"

"Yes, but–"

"Multiple hairs from a woman on your clothing, not yours. A sister seemed like your most likely flatmate."

"Extraordinary. You're just as I imagined from Dr. Watson's stories. When does my five minutes begin?"

"Right now."

"Very well." Miss Deeks cleared her throat. "I was born in Ontario in 1864. From my earliest youth, I have believed strongly that women can make a great contribution to the world's knowledge. I spent most of my third decade studying all over Europe, and I was finally able to enroll at the University of Toronto upon my return. After completing my education, I started teaching at Presbyterian Ladies' College."

"Miss Deeks, perhaps you should minimize your biographical details and focus at the crime you may be accused of committing."

"I'm getting there, Mr. Holmes, but if you're to understand, you must hear the story from the beginning. I've always been fascinated by history. Two decades ago I wrote a little article on the Women's Art Association of Canada, and through my work there and elsewhere, I got the idea to create a history of the world with special emphasis on the role that women have played in civilization since the beginning of recorded time. That's how I spent my war years, Mr. Holmes. I passed countless hours in the city's libraries, taking notes and honing my skills as a researcher. Then I finally got to work writing my book, and I finished it around the February before the war ended– 1918. I called it *The Web of the World's Romance*. The first book of its kind– a feminist history of the world."

Holmes believed that he was keeping his face impassive, but Miss Deeks seemed to detect something in his eyes. "Oh, I can see that such a book has no interest to you, Mr. Holmes. It didn't interest many publishers either. I met with editors, I sent them copies of my manuscript, and none of them believed that there was any market for *The Web*. In August of 1918, I sent a copy of my manuscript to the Macmillan Company, thinking they might be willing to publish it. They held onto the manuscript for nearly nine months. My hopes were very high, Mr. Holmes. Finally, they returned it to me, saying that they did not believe that my book could find an audience. I was very upset, and I didn't even unwrap the package containing the returned manuscript."

After glancing at the wall clock, Holmes sighed, saying, "Miss Deeks, you have two minutes remaining."

"Very well, Mr. Holmes. Have you read H.G. Wells' book *The Outline of History?*"

"I have not. I have heard of the volume, though."

"Very well. I first learned of Mr. Wells' *Outline* when I read a review of it, and I was thunderstruck. It sounded very much like my *Web*, in terms of scope and in other ways, so at my first opportunity I marched down to the department store and bought a copy. When I started reading it, I was stunned. My surprise turned to horror, and then to anger. Mr. Holmes, *The Outline* is based upon my *Web*. The general structure of the book, the events covered... it's all taken from my work!"

Holmes leaned forward. "Are you accusing Mr. Wells of plagiarism?"

"Yes! Yes, I am! Oh, he didn't copy my *Web* word for word, but he took what I said and rephrased it in his own style. I was so upset that I rushed back to the department store and demanded my money back for the book. This was a mistake, and I regretted it soon afterwards, so I had to go and buy another copy. But then I finally found the package containing the manuscript I'd sent to Macmillan and unwrapped it, and I was stunned. I expected the manuscript to possibly have a crease here and there, but the papers in that parcel were a mess. They were dog-eared, covered with stains, and heavily battered. It looked as if someone had been poring through it over and over again, not just for a cursory read-through, but to mine it for every scrap of information it contained. I compared my manuscript for *The Web* to Wells' *Outline*. It was amazing! The general narrative matched as if it were a stencil. So many of Wells' sentences were basically mine with a little bit of rewording. Oh, it made me furious! But the worst part was what Mr. Wells left out of his *Outline*! He deleted almost every reference I made to women's roles in history! He replaced them with his own musings on science and his denigration of religion and his predictions for the future of society."

Holmes stirred. "Miss Deeks, as you were both writing a history of the world, it's not surprising that you would both cover the same events."

"Yes, Mr. Holmes, that's true. But the point is that Mr. Wells also *overlooked the events that I ignored in my book*. Furthermore, I realized that I'd made a number of factual errors. Mr. Holmes, those exact factual errors are in *The Outline* as well!" Miss Deeks glanced at the clock. "My time is up. May I please continue?"

It would have been very easy for Holmes to have said "no," but the familiar stirrings of interest were arising, and despite himself he found himself wanting to hear more. "Five more minutes. The terms of the original deal will apply at the end of them."

"Thank you. I wasn't sure what to do, Mr. Holmes. I consulted with historians at universities, and they told me that I had a case for plagiarism. I kept up my comparison, finding every point of similarity, every match that was too close to be a coincidence. It was astounding, Mr. Holmes! It's like Mr. Wells couldn't be bothered to outline his own *Outline* and built upon my work instead. I spent several years showing the manuscript to respected historians, and they were amazed by the similarities. No publisher wanted to touch my book, largely because of Mr. Wells' book essentially having filled the market for a world history at this time. His *Outline* has become a massive bestseller, Mr. Holmes. He's made an absolute fortune from it!"

"And you think that you deserve a share of those profits, as you contend that he based his book on your scholarship without permission?"

"Yes, Mr. Holmes, I do. I am morally certain that the publishing company Macmillan sent my manuscript for *The Web* to Wells, and he used it as the basis of his own work. He claims to have written that massive two-volume work in only a year and a half. I don't believe that he could have done that level of research on his own, having done it myself. He had help, and he and the publishing house were so brazen that they thought that either I'd never learn about it, or that no one would believe me." Her lip trembled. "And hardly anybody outside of my own family has for twelve years now. A few years ago, right before the statute of limitations for filing a lawsuit passed, I sued Mr. Wells and Macmillan for plagiarizing my work and demanded credit and compensation."

"How much did you ask for, Miss Deeks?"

"Half a million Canadian dollars. Justice isn't cheap, Mr. Holmes. I am a woman of very limited means. Fortunately, I had a very generous and wealthy brother who thought it was his duty to support me in my litigation. Unfortunately, he passed away not long ago, and without his financial support I have been forced to deliver my appeals myself, without hired counsel."

"Then you have already received court judgments?"

"Yes. I filed in Ontario in 1928, but the judge, Justice– or rather, I should call him Mr. *Injustice* Raney– pooh-poohed all my claims without properly considering the evidence. He simply took the publishers and Mr. Wells' word, blithely declaring that they were honorable men and we could accept their word as gospel. I appealed, and to a man, the judges on the appellate panel upheld the previous unjust verdict. Everybody expected me to simply give up, but I remembered that several years ago, when the Canadian courts declared that women could not serve as senators because they were not legally considered persons under the law, that some determined women travelled across the Atlantic and filed suit in England, asking London's Privy Council to review the case. In that instance, Mr. Holmes, the Privy Council wisely threw out the previous verdict. I thought they might show similar good sense if I came to them. Unfortunately, with my brother gone and his widow and sons receiving all of his substantial wealth, I was left with just the little annuity he provided for me in his will. I have two sisters, Mr. Holmes. We got the use of a house for our lifetimes and six hundred dollars a year each. That's enough if you live very frugally. But in order to pursue my case, my sister Mabel and I had to move to London. We have found a very inexpensive hotel, and we make do on small rations. As I cannot afford a lawyer, I have put my own case forward in court. Unfortunately, just a couple of days ago– November 3rd, the judges ruled against me. They said that my evidence was not convincing, but I can't see how they can say that with a straight face!"

Holmes said nothing for a few moments, but once he realized that Miss Deeks needed a few moments to catch her breath, he remarked, "Then it seems that your legal battle is at an end, though it is not the conclusion that you would have hoped for, unfortunately."

"At an end? Hardly! I can assure you, Mr. Holmes, I have plenty of fight in me yet. I still have one more option available to me."

"But what can you do with the Privy Council ruling against you?"

"I can send a petition for assistance directly to the King. If he fulfills his duties as a monarch, he will see that one of his loyal subjects has been cruelly mistreated by the courts that are bound to administer his laws."

Holmes took a few moments to consider his reaction to his guest. There was something admirable in Miss Deeks' tenacity, though upon further reflection, he was uncertain as to whether this focus and drive was propelled by a thirst for justice or an unhealthy obsession. This woman was convinced that one of the most prominent authors in the world had utilized her work to propel the project that had made his fortune. It was small wonder that the judiciary had refused to consider that possibility. Holmes knew from experience that the courts were unwilling to question the word or the reputation of supposedly respectable men without adamantine proof of guilt.

"Are you asking me to find further proof of plagiarism, Miss Deeks?"

"What?" She looked rather stunned by this question. "No. I have no need of that. I believe that I have proven my case, and anybody who reads my report with an open mind can see at once that I am the victim of a particularly bold intellectual property theft." She reached into her bag and withdrew a thick sheaf of papers. "There's a copy of my report," she declared generously as she forced it into Holmes' reluctant hands. "You can read that at your leisure."

After a grunt that Miss Deeks chose to interpret as a "thank you," Holmes asked, "If you feel that you've made your own case plain, then I repeat, why did you come to me?"

"Because I'm afraid that I might be arrested for a murder I didn't commit!"

Holmes blinked. "Continue, please."

"Yesterday, a young woman came to my hotel room and told me that she believed that she had evidence that could prove that the publishers sent my manuscript to England, with the express intention of Mr. Wells reading it and building upon it for his own work. She claimed she used to work for the company in a secretarial capacity, and that she had a couple of memoranda that would prove my contentions beyond a shadow of a doubt."

"Did she ask for money, Miss Deeks?"

"Well, yes. She said that she had been fired for asking too many questions, and without a decent letter of reference she couldn't find another job."

"How much did she want? A hundred pounds? Two hundred?"

"Two hundred and fifty if you must know, Mr. Holmes."

"I must say, Miss Deeks, that is a considerable sum."

"My nephews would be happy to pay it if it meant that I could be vindicated."

"I see. And what is the name of this young woman?"

"Jane Jones. And before you say a word, Mr. Holmes, I am aware that it was a pseudonym. She was deathly afraid of repercussions."

"Very well. Describe Miss Jones, please."

"Young, I'd say no more than twenty-two. Reddish-gold hair, bobbed. Plenty of freckles, about five foot four."

"How are you supposed to get in touch with her?"

"I can't get in touch with her, Mr. Holmes. Not anymore. She's dead!"

The flames of interest were starting to burn much brighter in Holmes' mind. "Was this a homicide?"

"Yes! She told me to meet her at her friend's flat– really just a tiny room barely bigger than a closet in a rather seedy boarding house. Naturally I was suspicious. I do not claim to be an expert in crime and preventing oneself from being targeted by criminals. If I were, I would not have had to file my lawsuit. I was told to come alone, but I asked my sister Mabel to disguise herself and follow behind me. My sister was at the end of the corridor when I knocked on Miss Jones' door. There was no reply, but as the door wasn't locked, I pushed it open and saw Miss Jones lying on the floor with a bloodstain on her chest. I didn't even enter the room, and I saw no weapon. But then this woman– I never met her before and I don't know her name, came rushing out from behind the corner and started screaming, "What have you done! You've killed Jane!" I tried to tell her that she was utterly mistaken, but she kept howling, and I was afraid that I might be arrested, and that would completely destroy any chance of having my petition heard by the king. My sister grabbed my arm, and we made our escape. Luckily, that screaming woman didn't follow us."

"Very fortunate," Holmes murmured.

"Mr. Holmes, you look as if you've gotten an idea."

"Merely the germ of one, Miss Deeks."

"Would you care to share it?"

"No. It is dangerous to speculate upon insufficient evidence, and I shall need further information before venturing to express an opinion."

Pure joy seemed to radiate across Miss Deeks' face. "Then you will investigate?"

"The fate of Miss Jones, yes."

Miss Deeks observed that Holmes was not committing himself to looking into the plagiarism case and decided not to press her luck. "Thank you, Mr. Holmes! Thank you!"

"Please allow me twenty minutes to make some preparations. We will travel to London on the next available train."

As Miss Deeks sat quietly in Holmes' parlor, she heard him placing a telephone call, though she could not understand the words being said. Holmes eventually emerged wearing a suit styled for the city rather than the countryside, and carried a satchel.

The pair said little on the train. Every now and then Miss Deeks attempted to start a conversation, but all of her attempts produced minimal responses. When they finally disembarked at the station in London, a uniformed policeman walked straight up to them.

"Mr. Holmes, he's going to arrest me!" Miss Deeks shuddered.

"I very much doubt that. This is a friend of mine." As Holmes shook hands with the constable, he said, "Thank you for meeting us, Nestor."

"My pleasure, Holmes. It's good to have you back. Is there any chance of your resuming a permanent residence in London again?"

"None at all. I am quite content in my retirement."

"A great pity, sir. We really could use your help more often."

"You both flatter me and denigrate your colleagues. Am I correct in assuming that there is currently no warrant out for Miss Deeks?"

"No, sir. She's not wanted for murder."

"I'm not?" Miss Deeks' relief was obvious. "You know I didn't commit the crime?"

"Actually, ma'am, we're not sure there is a crime." As they talked, the three of them made their way out of the station. "No dead woman matching the description your provided has been found in the last twenty-four hours, Mr. Holmes. I examined the location you sent me to and found no corpse."

"And there was nothing of interest?"

"There was one thing, sir. I explored the alley behind the boarding house and found this." Nestor pulled a paper bag out from under his jacket. "As you'll soon see, there was a reason why I didn't consider it proper evidence."

As Holmes unwrapped the parcel and revealed the contents, Miss Deeks gasped. "That's the shirt Miss Jones was wearing!"

"And was the stain in this position?" Holmes turned the garment around to reveal a bright red oval.

"Yes! Is that her blood?"

"Almost certainly not. You will observe the intense crimson color, and the stained fabric is still quite soft and flexible. If this were actual blood, it would likely have darkened into a shade of brown, and what is more, the tainted cloth would have stiffened. Holmes held the stain to his nose and sniffed. "Vinegar and other chemicals. This is ink."

"Then Miss Jones isn't really dead?"

"I highly doubt it. She was feigning death, waiting for you to arrive. The woman who started screaming and accusing you of the murder was almost certainly an accomplice."

"But why would someone do that to me?"

"I can think of multiple reasons. One might be blackmail. You have very little money of your own, it is true, but you do have exceedingly wealthy nephews who inherited a fortune from your brother. If you absolutely needed the funds, you could almost certainly rely on them for a certain level of financial support. Someone could conceivably make a considerable profit from placing you in a position where you'd gladly pay to avoid arrest."

"You don't look convinced, Mr. Holmes."

"That's because it's too risky. It would take a while to get the money, and how much could really be expected? Of course, in my time I have known confidence tricksters to go to astounding lengths to cheat gullible people out of a few shillings, but I am particularly struck by the fact that the screaming, accusing woman didn't follow you out the door to stop you, nor was your flight impeded by another member of the conspiracy." Holmes shook his head. "That leads to an alternative explanation. The situation was meant to get you to flee. The goal of this whole rigmarole was to get you to flee England at once and return to Canada in order to avoid arrest and public censure. By doing so, this entire lawsuit would be permanently put to rest."

"But who would be behind it?" Miss Deeks demanded. "Mr. Wells? The publisher?"

"Unknown at present. It will require more information, and I hope to get it from an interview I have in just under an hour."

"Who are you meeting, Mr. Holmes?"

"H.G. Wells, of course. By a lucky coincidence, he's giving a lecture at a museum tonight, and some colleagues of mine were able to help me make an appointment with him."

"I'd like to come with you," Miss Deeks sighed, "but I don't think that Mr. Wells would take too kindly to my presence."

"Meaning no offense, I completely agree. I suggest that you return to your hotel and assure your sister that you are all right. In the meantime, I've arranged for someone I know to wait outside your room as your bodyguard. If my theory is correct, someone tried to drive you out of England, and it's possible that they may be impatient to get results. If so, then there's a slight but very real chance that you might be in danger, so a protector's presence will minimize that risk."

Holmes had feared that Miss Deeks would resent the presence of a man watching over them, but to his relief, she quickly acquiesced. After she left with Nestor as her escort, Holmes made his way to the British Museum, where he was led to a small room down the corridor from the hall where Wells would deliver a speech in a short while.

Wells professed himself delighted to meet Holmes, and the first few minutes of their conversation was devoted to Wells asking questions about some of Holmes' scientific discoveries, as well as Holmes' thoughts on various international questions. Holmes was pleased to talk about his forensic experiments, but was largely uninterested in politics. After he sensed that Wells was properly relaxed in the conversation, Holmes explained the reason for the meeting. Taking great care not to say anything that might potentially antagonize Wells, Holmes explained the situation of Miss Deeks and the faked murder, and deftly tried to convey that he did not suspect Wells of having anything to do with it while carefully not actually committing himself to a position on the matter.

Holmes had presented the situation adroitly, and Wells did not appear the least bit antagonized. "So, you think some unscrupulous criminals are trying to profit from this ridiculous lawsuit?" Wells asked.

"That certainly is possible," Holmes replied blandly.

"Hmm, it makes sense to me. Why would just one deluded old woman try to pick my pocket? Why wouldn't others try their luck as well?" Wells shook his head. "Just as I think that this whole situation is finally put to bed, that woman keeps finding another way to prolong the inconvenience."

"I can see how this whole situation can be distressing for you."

"I'm not worried about it. I know there's nothing to her claims and I've always been quite confident that the courts will see the situation clearly. I've never had the slightest doubt about that. Still, the legal fees are an annoyance. Goodness knows I can afford them, especially after my royalties from *The Outline*, but still, I hate to see my bank account drained unnecessarily. I've instructed my attorneys to pursue recoupment of costs, you know. They're considering a forced bankruptcy, or finding a way to break the annuity her brother left her in order to take the costs from the principal. The fees are running up to three or four thousand pounds by now."

"Surely that would ruin Miss Deeks," Holmes noted.

Wells shrugged. "Her brother was a millionaire. Her relatives will look after her. Anyway, what sort of precedent would that set if I just let the matter lie? Every Tom, Dick, and Harry would scribble together a manuscript based on my latest book and claim I'd taken their idea. The only way to vindicate myself and save myself future headaches is to make it clear to the world that false allegations will only impoverish you."

"Do you bear Miss Deeks much ill will?"

"Not at all," Wells waved his hand and laughed. "I feel rather sorry for her, as a matter of fact. Elderly woman, repressed– never married. Never got a chance to explore the womanly aspects of her character, I suspect. Not a bad woman, just a deluded one. A little…" Wells placed a finger to his temple and started tracing circles on the side of his head. "She's not a well woman, you know. Clearly delusional. Fancies herself a great writer and historian. I actually think she really believes that she wrote my book. I don't know if she found my book and wrote a manuscript based on it, or if she actually tried to write a history of the world and produced that laughable result, but it's all the ravings of a ridiculous old woman. Her relatives really ought to have taken her aside long ago and made it clear that she can't just sling false allegations like that, but as I said, I think she really believes them now. It's sad, really. She's sinking into her dotage, looking back at a life full of missed opportunities, and she's desperate to grab a little glory in the twilight of her years. Unfortunately, she just happened to fixate on me. But I can't really be angry at her. It's pity I feel."

Holmes carefully asked a few more questions, but Wells was unable to provide him with any more useful information. When Wells announced his need to end the interview and begin preparations for his talk, the two men shook hands and Holmes took his leave.

The next item on Holmes' agenda was to speak to someone familiar with Wells who might be able to provide some information as to whether the author or a colleague of his might have been involved in the faked murder. One of Holmes' many sources who kept a close eye on the comings and goings of London's citizenry had suggested a pair of prominent authors who were currently sharing a meal at a local pub. A quick journey a mile and a half east, and Holmes found himself at a brightly lit and pleasant establishment. Sitting in the corner were an enormous man with a great cape and pince-nez, and a much smaller man seated next to him. Both men had platters of bacon and eggs in front of them, with bread and cheese on a board between them, and tankards of beer as well.

The larger man saw Holmes approaching and immediately rose. "Sherlock Holmes! How wonderful to see you again!"

Holmes gripped the hand of G.K. Chesterton, and then similarly greeted Hilaire Belloc. "The pleasure's all mine. It's been a year since we last met, hasn't it? When our mutual friend, Father Brown and I were wrapping up the case of the Blood of Hailes."

"I believe so, yes." Chesterton pushed the board of bread and cheese to Holmes and indicated that he should help himself. "Of course, I completely understand why this story can't be revealed to the general public for quite some time, given the nature of the scandal you unearthed, but the manuscript will remain in my lawyer's strongbox for at least ninety years."

"Thank you for your understanding, Chesterton. If it were up to me, the world would know exactly what happened, but a great many innocent people might be harmed by the release of the details of that case. I thank you for your discretion as Father Brown's literary agent."

Belloc took a sip from his tankard. "So Holmes, what are you doing back in London? A case of some kind?"

"Yes. It involves a mutual acquaintance of ours. H.G. Wells."

Belloc's eyebrows arched. "Please, tell us more."

Holmes summarized the story of Miss Deeks' visit and the mysterious death that was very likely a hoax. By the end of it, Chesterton appeared thoughtful and Belloc looked triumphant.

"I heard rumors about the lawsuit against Wells, but the newspapers have been suspiciously reticent in providing details."

"You appear to take pleasure in hearing the details of Miss Deeks' argument, Belloc."

"It's not pleasure so much as vindication, and I can only hope that Miss Deeks is able to discredit Wells' *Outline* even further than I have."

"You have issues with the book?" Holmes wondered.

"I most certainly do. It's an impressive tome until Wells starts covering the history of humanity, which means that it all falls apart at about page seven. It's a monolithic mishmash of false assumptions, stretched-out half-truths, and outright bigotry. It's not a proper exploration of the history of the world, it's a chopped-up, twisted, and distorted vision of Wells trying to remake several millennia in his own image."

Chesterton chuckled. "I believe that Wells once compared debating with Belloc to arguing with a hailstorm."

"If only I were an actual hailstorm, perhaps I could knock some sense into him. The entire book is a malicious sneer against religion in general, particularly Christianity. The life of Christ is barely given any attention. Ancient Greco-Persian battles receive more ink and paper that Jesus. Wells has the very grievous fault of being ignorant that he is ignorant. He has the strange cocksuredness of the man who knows only the old conventional textbook of his schooldays and mistakes it for universal knowledge."

"Try to not to sugarcoat your thoughts," Chesterton murmured with a small smile.

"You and I have a very different approach to intellectual battle with our opponents," Belloc said with an indignant sniff. "You've managed to maintain your friendship with Wells despite your differences. He and I will remain at loggerheads until one of us dies. Our literary rejoinders reflect our contrasting styles."

"Literary rejoinders? I was not aware that you'd written books in response to Wells' *Outline*," Holmes remarked.

"Oh, yes. Chesterton produced a wonderful volume titled *The Everlasting Man*," Belloc explained, "which put a proper focus on the benefits and cultural impact that Christ has had on the last nineteen hundred years. And our mutual friend was very polite in his introduction. What was that you said, Gilbert?"

"I may not be quoting myself word for word, but I believe I wrote, "*As I have more than once differed from Mr. H. G. Wells in his view of history, it is the more right that I should here congratulate him on the courage and constructive imagination which carried through his vast and varied and intensely interesting work; but still more on having asserted the reasonable right of the amateur to do what he can with the facts which the specialists provide.*" Wells was much like a writer who didn't care for the protagonist of his book–which is why he marginalized Jesus so much in it."

"Very civilized. Would you like to hear what I wrote in my articles, Holmes?"

"I would. Even if I didn't, I don't believe I'd be able to stop you."

"You would not. I wrote two dozen articles ripping his specious arguments and misplaced assertions to shreds. I put them together into a combined volume titled *A Companion to Mr. Wells' "Outline of History."* Wells didn't like that one bit. He wrote several articles in reply, but couldn't find anybody to print them until he put them together into a book titled *Mr. Belloc Objects to "The Outline of History."* He said my "apparent arrogance is largely the protection of a fundamentally fearful man," and that I am "the sort of man who talks loud and fast for fear of hearing the other side.""

"How did you reply to that, Belloc?"

Belloc took another sip of beer. "I wrote one more book critiquing his poor arguments and titled it *Mr. Belloc Still Objects.*"

"You had so much to criticize that you were able to fill two books?" Holmes asked.

"Well, the second book is rather short. You know, Wells' work is full of silly mistakes. On one page, he said that early humans had no knowledge of arrow-firing bows, only to show reproductions of cave paintings with the figures holding archery weapons later. When Wells wrote his response to me, he opened his volume by declaring that he was "the least controversial of men." Perhaps he was sincere, and perhaps his tongue was firmly affixed to his cheek."

Holmes hesitated before asking his next questions. "You two are acquainted with Wells. I can assure you that your opinions will not go no further than this table. Do you give any credence to the allegations of plagiarism, and do you think that Wells could have had anything to do with this attempt to frighten Miss Deeks out of England?"

Chesterton stroked his chin. "As for the question of whether he would fake a murder to drive Miss Deeks away, I would say not. Wells is a confident man, and I'm quite certain he has complete faith in the courts to rule in his favor, especially seeing as how everything has gone completely his way so far. He has triumphed multiple times with the use of lawyers, he has no need to devise dramatic scenes in order to end the litigation. In any event, from what you've told us, Wells actually wants to initiate further legal proceedings in order to recoup his costs. If he wanted Miss Deeks out of his life, he could just forget the money and not jump through the additional hoops of forced bankruptcy. I believe he could afford the loss."

"And what about the allegations of plagiarism?"

Chesterton hesitated. "I will not say anything potentially defamatory against a man I consider a friend. I will, however, say that I do *not* believe that Miss Deeks is a hysterical woman and that I think that attempts to paint her as such are unfair. There is one more rumor I've heard... I'm not sure if you're aware of this, but I've heard through some colleagues that there was a minor scandal some years back regarding the Canadian branch of the publishing house in question. It was a case very much like Miss Deeks'. A woman wrote a monograph on some aspect of astronomy, I don't remember which. She submitted it to the publishing house, which rejected it after a substantial period of time. Then, the publishers soon produced another work on astronomy, and the woman started alleging that her manuscript had been plundered and repurposed."

Holmes' eyes widened. "The same editors? Essentially the same allegations?"

"Quite a coincidence, isn't it?" Belloc noted. "An unknown writer produces an educational text. The publishers already have a much more prominent author at work on a similar subject, but they realize that the production of their preferred author's work could be substantially sped up using this obscure writer's manuscript as a template. A few changes, deletions, expansions, and a reworking by a much more gifted prose stylist, and they could have a bestseller on their hands."

"Indeed. I now would like your thoughts on those same questions, Belloc."

"I think I answered the first one with my recent comments. Wells paints himself as a fearless advocate of women's emancipation, but is he really? His wife– his *second* wife, Catherine, their relationship was the cause of his divorce from his first wife. And poor departed Catherine. Do you know what he called her? Jane! He gave her that name because it represents the epitome of domesticity and loyalty to him. He refused to call her by her true name, and for all their marriage he forced her to play the role he demanded of her. He took away her true name, the name she loved, and forced her to play the role of the uncomplaining, efficient house-manager whose only whim was to support his careers and desires." Belloc took a deep breath. "And there was no shortage of women during his marriage to Catherine. The most famous name is probably that birth control woman, Margaret Sanger. It's been my experience that the men who are the most outspoken champions of women's equality are often the men who treat women most cruelly."

"Be careful of wandering into the realms of gossip," Chesterton warned.

"Then let's return to the realms of literary criticism. The first books that pop into the average person on the street's mind when they think of Wells are his science fiction novels. In truth, he's hardly penned anything in that genre since around the turn of the century. Most of his fiction has been realistic domestic fare, featuring a brilliant, misunderstood man who can only find happiness and fulfillment through his extramarital affairs, and he's continually thwarted by the oppressive demands of society, though he is often buttressed by an understanding wife, who sympathizes with him even if she cannot satisfy him. This is a recurring theme of many of Wells' novels over the last few decades. Are the protagonists of these novels all self-portraits? The critics can debate this for years."

After a moment's pause, Belloc added. "There's one more point. Earlier in his career, Wells was accused of plagiarizing another author's work. I believe that case was settled somehow."

Holmes mulled over all of this for a few moments until the silence was broken by Chesterton.

"Have you spoken to Miss Mabel Deeks?" Chesterton asked. "Speaking of women, I would say that if something's been going on, she'd be a sharp observer. Perhaps she noted something that Miss Florence missed."

"That is an excellent point. I should speak to her immediately."

Holmes was true to his word, and soon afterwards, he was speaking to the Deeks sisters in their hotel room. "Miss Mabel, have you noticed anything unusual lately?"

"I'm not sure what you mean, Mr. Holmes. Everything's a bit unusual. London life is rather different from living in Ontario in many ways."

"Have you noticed anything that might potentially be connected to a criminal action?"

"If I had, I would have reported it, Mr. Holmes," Mabel Deeks replied virtuously.

"My sister is an observant and intelligent woman," Florence noted. "If she'd seen something amiss, we'd know."

"Sometimes, the most important details are the ones that we don't attach much significance at the time," Holmes explained.

"Well, I've been having restless nights, and I've been hearing all sorts of odd noises around bedtime, but that's probably due to the brandy."

"What brandy?"

"My sister and I are not habitual imbibers, Mr. Holmes, but since we moved to this hotel, we've found it necessary to take a little nip of brandy every night before we retire," Florence Deeks explained. "The building is not well-insulated, and taken strictly for medicinal purposes, a bit of spirits helps keep out the cold during the chilly nights."

"But I don't respond well to it," Mabel Deeks mourned. "It makes me come out in gooseflesh all over. It affects my sleep, and I keep hearing noises that are probably just my imagination. Last week, around midnight, I heard some clomping noises and thought there was a horse galloping down the hall. I hurried out and didn't even think to put on my dressing-gown. I saw a man rushing out the door at the end of the corridor, and I saw something slip out of his pocket and roll away into that corner under the table there, but before I could call him back, it was too late. He was gone. And I've seen– or thought I've seen– people coming in and out of that room across from ours at all hours of the night. Many's the time I've looked out when I've heard a noise at one or two in the morning and seen somebody with the face of a ghost there."

"Why haven't I seen those people?" Florence Deeks demanded.

"You've been sleeping sounder than I have."

"Did you check under that table for the dropped item?" Holmes asked.

"No, sir. It slipped my mind, and anyway, at my age, my knees aren't what they used to be."

Holmes had a quick word with Nestor, who was still standing guard outside. A moment later he returned with a small phial in one hand. "It must've rolled right behind the leg of the table," Nestor explained.

Holmes took it from him, uncorked the top, and sniffed it. "Cocaine," he pronounced.

"Are you sure, Mr. Holmes?" Florence Deeks wondered.

"Believe me, I know. A rather weak one, I believe. No more than a four percent solution." Holmes replaced the phial's stopper and handed it back to Nestor. "The room directly across from yours, you said, Miss Mabel?"

"Yes, that's right."

"I see. We shall have to find different accommodations for you tonight. I believe that the police will need this room for an investigation."

That night, a team of Scotland Yard officers waited inside the Deeks sisters' hotel room, and after a brief period of observation, noticed several figures entering and leaving the room across the hall. When stopped and searched on their way out of the hotel, they were all carrying phials containing solutions of cocaine.

The next day, Holmes explained the entire situation to the Deeks sisters. "You mean we've been living across the hall from drug-sellers?" an indignant Florence asked.

"It appears so, yes. We'll need you to make some identifications…"

An hour later, Florence identified two women who had been arrested in connection with the case as Jane Jones and the woman who had accused her of the murder.

"None of this had anything whatsoever to do with the lawsuit," Holmes explained, "aside from the fact that your participation in the litigation meant that you had to take up residence at this hotel. The gang moved their distribution centers about frequently, but this was a particularly convenient location for them. Most hotel staff and residents studiously ignore the goings-on of the residents, but when Miss Mabel's nocturnal observations became more frequent, the gang decided that to avoid suspicion, they needed to get rid of her."

"But they didn't try to kill me!"

"No. A murder would have only drawn attention to this location, and the best course of action was to drive you and your sister from the hotel. They did a little background research on you, learned about the lawsuit, and decided that if they could lure Miss Florence somewhere and frighten her with being accused of murder, you'd take the next ship back to Canada. They reasoned that you were low on funds, and hoped you were sufficiently demoralized to give up the lawsuit as a bad job. They thought that your experiences would crush any faith you had in the British justice system, making you all the more willing to flee."

"They didn't know me well at all," Florence Deeks sniffed. "So this whole affair was all about Mabel? She was the dangerous witness they wanted out the country, and they had no interest whatsoever in the lawsuit?"

"Precisely."

"Thank you, Mr. Holmes." Florence Deeks sighed. "I regret that I lack the funds to recompense you for your assistance, but perhaps if I speak to my nephews–"

"There will be no fee," Holmes assured her.

"I see. Well, if anybody can find evidence of plagiarism that will convince the King, it's you, but I cannot ask you to continue working for me for free. My sense of honor will not allow me to accept any more charity from a man who has already been very generous to me." Florence Deeks spoke with firm finality.

"What do you intend to do now, Miss Deeks?"

"What I have been doing for the last several years, Mr. Holmes. I will see this through to the end, and I will appeal directly to the King, and hope that our monarch, in his wisdom, will see fit to reopen the case and encourage to look at the evidence with fresh and unprejudiced eyes. I will not deny that the odds are against me, but a high chance of failure is not reason to refrain from continuing in a righteous cause."

"And no matter what happens, Florence will have me right by her side," Mabel Deeks added. "We've been investigating this together for over a decade. There's nothing in the world that can convince us to give this up now. No matter what happens, we'll keep telling the world what we know is the truth."

"I see." Holmes rose to his feet. "Then as my role in this case appears to be completed, I shall return home to my bees. My very best wishes to both of you!"

(Author's note: Other than Holmes, the only fictional characters in this story are Nestor, Jane Jones, and the other unnamed characters involved in the drug gang. All of the other characters and events are real, and are portrayed as true to life as possible.

Florence Deeks' appeal to the King was rejected, and with all of her options exhausted, and their finances strained to the breaking point, Florence and Mabel returned to Canada. Florence outlived Wells by thirteen years and died in 1959 at the age of ninety-four. She continued writing, including another work of history centered on the achievements of women, but none of her work was ever published, and her papers were archived in Canada.

They remained there until the historian A.B. (Alexander Brian) McKillop researched and wrote his book <u>The Spinster and the Prophet: Florence Deeks, H.G. Wells, and the Mystery of the Purloined Past</u>, published in 2002. This book was a central source for the background research for this story, and many of the words spoken by Wells, Chesterton, and Belloc are the authors' own words, taken from their writings, Wikipedia articles, and essays by Dale Ahlquist, Karl Keating, and Joseph Pearce. I first learned about this case by reading Robert Evans' 2009 <u>Cracked</u> article "5 Great Men Who Built Their Careers on Plagiarism."

McKillop's work is sympathetic to Deeks, though his research did not produce a "smoking gun" of plagiarism. The many similarities between the works are undeniable, but that is not conclusive evidence of Wells' guilt. There is one possibility that has not been looked into to the best of my knowledge– forensic analysis. If the original manuscript of Deeks' Web is safely housed in the archives, there is an outside chance that century-old fingerprints, preserved in ink or grease, might remain on the manuscript. The best place to look would be the dog-eared corners of the papers. Of course, handling by archivists and researchers may have obliterated some evidence, and the detection of fingerprints (or even DNA from traces of sweat or perhaps a licked fingertip) is worthless without fingerprint records or DNA indisputable from Wells to compare against carefully. To the best of my knowledge, there are currently no plans to analyze the manuscript for such evidence, but if by some remote chance an inky partial fingerprint was found on the underside of a dog-eared corner and it could be matched, it might disprove Wells' assertions that he never saw Florence Deeks' manuscript. An absence of forensic evidence would certainly be a point in Wells' favor, but it would not disprove Deeks' claims. Barring a long-hidden written confession by one of the parties involved in the case, it's unlikely that this historical mystery will ever be solved to everybody's satisfaction. This remains a highly controversial topic, with

supporters of both Wells and Deeks taking strong stances on opposite
sides of the debate.)